THE ROGUE GOD

CONNOR WHITELEY

No part of this book may be reproduced in any form or by any electronic or mechanical means. Including information storage, and retrieval systems, without written permission from the author except for the use of brief quotations in a book review.

This book is NOT legal, professional, medical, financial or any type of official advice.

Any questions about the book, rights licensing, or to contact the author, please email connorwhiteley@connorwhiteley.net

Copyright © 2023 CONNOR WHITELEY

All rights reserved.

DEDICATION
Thank you to all my readers without you I couldn't do what I love.

PART ONE: THE SUPERHERO PSYCHOLGIST

CONNOR WHITELEY

CHAPTER 1

As I leant against the cold brick wall of one of the many little shops in Canterbury high street with its cobblestone ground, little cafes everywhere and plenty of university students, I just watched people go about their business in the busy university city.

The air was amazingly fresh with the hints of pine, designer coffee from the local coffee shops and the strange combination of all the wonderful brands of aftershave and perfumes the students wore. That all combined to leave a strange, but rather pleasant, taste of refreshing mint on my tongue.

I always had loved Canterbury that little historic city in the south of England that no one actually cared about, remembered or did too much with. But I had gone to university, lost my virginity here too and just fell in love with the city.

So when I became a superhero in the counselling and therapy sector, I knew exactly where I wanted to return to. I had to come back to the place I love, and with there being three universities close by, I just knew that there would never be a shortage of people who needed my help.

It really just makes me smile now, because before I became a superhero I was a mental health doctor and worked for the National Health Service, but the amount of myths and stigma and other awful things I faced on a daily basis was ridiculous.

All because people believed psychology wasn't a real science and therapy was useless, and I was only good at profiling people.

Hell! Psychology isn't profiling. Profiling is shit.

But I really do laugh at it all now, because it turned out that a bunch of my superhero powers are versions of the psychology myths. And they are pretty cool. I can know everything about a person just by what they say, I can read their minds and I can influence them if I really want to.

Being a superhero is great!

So that was what I was doing today, I was simply walking around Canterbury wanting to find someone who needed my help. Of course, I always hoped when I went out that I wouldn't find anyone. I always had hated seeing people in pain.

But there were always people needing my help.

As all the young university students laughed and talked and listened to the street musicians, I couldn't help but start to feel like something was off ever so slightly.

I focused on all the people walking up and down

the high street and noticed that one particular man in the crowd was giving off a slightly red aura.

That was definitely still a superpower I was getting used to, seeing people's auras was still so strange to me, but I was sure that this person was in deep trouble.

I slowly started to glide through the crowd towards him and I just stopped. A few people bumped into me and started to look annoyed but I just focused on my smile and that seemed to make them happy, so they went on with their day.

I stepped back out of the crowd so I wouldn't bump into anyone else, and I was right. I recognised that particular man with his middle-aged fit body, long black beard and expensive look. He was another superhero, yes, he worked in the Gambling Sector.

I couldn't remember for the life of me what his name was, but I had worked with him decades ago on helping a young woman off her gambling addiction. But I couldn't understand why this man wasn't okay.

And the red aura was still troubling.

Normally when people were sad, annoyed or depressed they just looked it and my superpowers would direct me in their direction. There was none of this red aura stuff.

So why was he giving off a red aura and what did it mean?

With me being a relatively new superhero (at least when compared to those who had been one since ancient times), I just knew that I was going to need help, superhero help.

"Octavia!" I shouted.

A few people looked at me weirdly and I quickly realised that I had to stop doing that in public.

But a few moments later everyone around me sort of became blurry and then one of the most stunning women I had ever seen just appeared, and everyone in the high street just acted like she had always been there.

Now I was definitely into both men and women, and whilst I seriously leant more towards men most of the time, Octavia was definitely one of those women that made me question myself. She was that stunning.

I had always loved her stunningly fit body without an ouch of body fat, her long wavy brown hair and just her smile. Believe me that smile could honestly melt the icecaps without any help from global warming.

So yea, she really was that stunning, and damn well hot.

"Matilda darling," Octavia said with a massive smile.

Octavia was probably the first ever superhero I met decades ago during my own transformation into a full superhero. She had worked in a few different sectors of the superhero world, and now I knew she was currently working in the Gambling Sector and helped out there.

If anyone would know what was going on with

that red aura man it would be Octavia. So I just pointed to him, and Octavia's face just dropped.

"Well my darling that is hardly a good aura," Octavia said. "I had heard a rumour he was bad…"

Then Octavia just started to look me up and down and smiled. God, that smile could make me do anything.

"Matilda darling, are you free for a little helping?" Octavia asked.

I just smiled. "What's going on?"

Octavia gestured us to glide into the crowd and walk with everyone else as we spoke, but I knew she wanted to stay close to the red aura man. I just didn't know why.

"His name is Jaxon Ellis. A Superhero in the Gambling sector, a very good one from what I heard but he has a problem…,"

I just shook my head. Saying that people had problems was so horrible, demeaning and so last century. Modern day mental health preferred to describe that as difficulties, since these "problems" were just a part of a person, but they should be changed to help them have less "problematic" behaviour.

But I decided this wasn't the time for details with sexy Octavia.

"Is that why you started working with the Gambling Sector?" I asked.

Octavia nodded. "Yes Jaxon went missing, superhero worked needed to be done so I stepped up,"

"What is his difficulty?" I asked.

A few people bumped into us and knocked Octavia into my arms, that was a very pleasurable accident. She quickly stood up and got back to walking with the crowd.

Shame.

"He has what professional gamblers call a leak,"

I bit my lip and nodded. I had treated plenty of gambling addicts over the decades in my practice and I had come to understand that there was real skill involved in poker, and you could actually win a lot of money playing it.

Yet you were stupid to try and play and win at blackjack, the slot machines and the other games in casinos where the house would rig the odds in its favour. That's why professional gamblers never played those sorts of games.

Clearly Jaxon wasn't as professional as I thought, and it was clearly affecting his mental health.

"How much has he lost?" I asked.

"He's homeless. His kids and parents and wife won't talk to him and he is about to be fired as a superhero,"

I just stopped dead in my tracks. Lots of people bumped into and swore but I used my calming superpowers to make them happy.

I pulled Octavia against a window of a small supermarket near the edge of the high street.

Before now I didn't know that could actually

happen, superheroes were superheroes. I didn't think we could get fired or anything.

"How do I help him?" I asked.

Octavia frowned. Damn even with her frowning she was hot as hell.

"He is another one of your... clients as you like to call them. Treat him and see if he wants to get better. Then call me with your results,"

With that everyone round me became blurry once more and then Octavia was gone. I always liked it how easy and straight forward people made therapy sound, but even as a superhero it still took time.

I looked back into the crowd of people and saw Jaxon was lighting a cigarette and walking towards me. His red aura started to get bigger and bigger and darker.

Then as he stood next to me I instantly recognised the smell as weed. He wasn't just smoking a cigarette, he was trying to get stoned.

I went over to him and gently tapped his shoulder.

I didn't always need people to talk to me to be able to analyse them and see all their thoughts. And all I had expected to see in Jaxon's mind was some gambling difficulties, a need for thrills and maybe something going on in his personal life.

But this was something else. Jaxon was a massive drug addict and I was amazed he wasn't brain dead with the amount of weed he smoked every day. But that's why he loved being a superhero because it took tons of weed to start affecting him. Then he used his poker winnings to buy drugs, and when they weren't enough he started to play the slots to get more.

Yet he only lost.

"What ya prob girl?" Jaxon said, clearly starting to get stoned.

I focused my calming and trusting superpowers on him, and he slowly started to look at me like a friend.

"You really should stop doing drugs," I said softly.

With my hand still on his shoulder I felt my minor command sink into his mind but his face didn't look impressed. He didn't want to stop doing drugs, and as much as I wanted to do properly therapy with him I really didn't like the colour of his aura.

It seemed like the more he smoked the red it got. And even the aura was starting to turn black around the edges.

Black meant death.

CHAPTER 2

As much as I didn't want to even start to admit it, I was really starting to believe that Jaxon was going to die or end himself by tomorrow morning.

I almost couldn't blame him. He had no friends left in the superhero world, his family refused to talk to him and he was in extreme amounts of gambling debt. He had nothing to live for.

So I decided I needed to try a more direct path.

"I'm Matilda Plum, superhero in the Counselling and Therapy Sector," I said extending my hand.

Jaxon's eyes looked a little distant but he barely managed to shake my hand.

"Jaxon, superhero of… I donno. A sector,"

"People are worried about you Jaxon. They love you so why don't you tell me why you'll doing this destruction to yourself,"

Jaxon seemed to frown and smile and want to cry at the minor reminder of the damage he had caused. I focused my superpowers on making him want to feel like he wanted to change his ways.

"I just needed the thrills," he said. "Poker gets old quickly. I wanna smoke,"

He just started laughing as he smoked more and more. I knew I was going to have to do something a bit extreme but I didn't feel like I had another option.

I focused every ounce of influencing superpower to make him feel sick whenever he thought, looked or tasted any sort of drug, even caffeine.

Extreme I know, but I had to save him from himself.

He just started coughing and stamped out the cigarette. His aura only started to get darker and darker around the edges.

Then I implanted the suggestion of all the superheroes that were missing him, caring about him and wanted him to be okay deep into his mind.

He slowly smiled. "They really care about me?"

I wrapped an arm around his shoulder. "Of course. They're worried sick about you. They just want you to be okay and back being the amazing superhero you were,"

As Jaxon just stared out into space for a few moments, I wondered if the drugs had already taken affect too well. But he just sort of smiled and nodded.

"I want to see them too," Jaxon said. "What I need to do?"

I folded my arms and wondered about that myself. His difficulty was clearly caused by the drugs and gambling so if I could get him away completely from all of that for a while, so we could work on the other causes and anything else that might be causing his addiction. Then that would work.

He would have to be away from the internet (online poker), other people and everything else that could possibly make him relapse whilst he focused on me and his recovery. But it could work.

I actually might even know a great place we could stay for a while.

"You know," I said to Jaxon, "my boss Natalia, the Goddess of Counselling and Therapy, owns a wonderful villa on the coast of Italy we could stay for a month or two for your therapy. There's plenty of sun, sand and that sea view is just stunning,"

Jaxon really looked like he was going to hate it, and I honestly thought he was going to say no. But he started nodding, still frowning and gestured that he should get going.

"You sure you want to help your addiction?" I asked.

"Of course. I want to be back with my superhero friends and helping them out," he said.

But I just couldn't believe his heart was in it entirely, yet as a superhero, I had to try and help him as much as I could. Even if his heart wasn't completely in it.

CHAPTER 3

Now I had wanted to spend two months with Jaxon in that wonderful Italian villa so we could work on everything. And I mean everything! But that seriously hadn't happened and I was rather furious actually.

I walked into Octavia's large black office that was decorated in wonderful black tones, pictures of famous poker games and she was sitting at her massive black desk. I had to admit she looked stunning, sexy and just perfect in her little red dress that made her look so dangerous and alluring.

"Matilda darling, this is unexpected," Octavia said.

I just frowned at her. I always had a rule whenever I did these sorts of things with people like Jaxon. The rule was simple, they could leave at any time, because I was a therapist, I was not a prison guard.

But that always became risky when I was dealing

with people as… "problematic" as Jaxon.

"Not in the slightest," I said. "His drug and gambling addiction is far worse than I ever imagined, and there is a reason why he doesn't want to stay,"

Octavia leant closer. "Why?"

"Because whenever people come to therapy, they have to be willing to change their behaviours because it is their behaviour that is causing the *problem*. Jaxon will never change or be willing to change,"

Octavia folded her arms. "You've done everything you can,"

My eyebrows rose. I was so used to being questioned in my methods because I had a *psychology* degree I didn't know why I still reacted, but I had to admit it did hurt each and every time someone questioned me for no good reason.

I nodded.

Octavia stood there and then paced round her office for a few moments.

"Thank you," Octavia said with a killer smile. "Me, the other Gambling Superheroes and the God of Gambling himself thanks you,"

"What will happen to him?" I asked. "I've already dropped him off at a casino in London because he demanded it,"

Octavia kept smiling at me, and I couldn't help but feel like it was the sort of smile you give someone you wanted to do… and hard.

"I will report to the God of Gambling and he will most properly fire Jaxon and make him a normal person again," Octavia said before she disappeared.

I just wished I could do something else, this felt like such a failure, but I could honestly say I had tried everything with Jaxon.

But he just didn't want to change.

Two weeks later I was walking along the wonderful cobblestone high street of Canterbury on a breathtakingly warm evening with the sounds of musicians playing, students drinking and talking when I got the news.

Jaxon Ellis had been found dead by a heroin overdose a few hours before, and as the air was filled with great hints of alcohol, rich Italian food and freshly baked garlic bread. I knew that there was nothing that I could have done.

You see as a therapist and superhero, it is my job to do my best with whoever I have to deal with. I love it. I get to help people improve their lives, stop their distress and help them in ways no one else can.

99% of the time, the job was amazing and it was more like play rather than work. Because it was so fun and I absolutely loved it.

But it was days like this when my hard "work" didn't pay off that honestly just felt shitty. And like everything I did just didn't matter and I was nothing more than a failure.

Yet I was never that. I always did my best, helped tons of people and most of all I allowed people to make their own choices. With all my superpowers I could easily bend people to my will, but I didn't.

Because it was wrong and I really do believe in one particular therapy concept.

Everyone has to have a capacity to change.

And Jaxon Ellis did not.

He didn't want to help his addiction, so he was always going to end up like this sadly. I truly hated that fact.

But as I started to walk along the high street again, looking for someone else to help, I just knew there would be another time, another person, another opportunity to help someone.

And that time I would be able to. All because that person would have a capacity to change.

CHAPTER 4

Bloody hell, let me tell you being a superhero on a very drunk night out is amazing. Not only can you drink a lot, lot more before you start to be seriously drunk but you get no hangover the next morning.

Brilliant!

So as I sat on a very comfortable black chair around a little glass table on the top level of an extremely packed night club. I was definitely starting to feel a little drunk, the night club wasn't moving too much, but I doubt I could walk too much in a straight line.

It was amazingly fun being a superhero and drunk. Especially because my superpowers also went a little… weird let's call it. Like one of my superpowers was to influence people in minor, subtle ways. So when I found an extremely hot guy and wished he took his white dress shirt off.

He did.

And boy, oh boy it was worth the unethical

behaviour. His chest and body looked like it belonged to a Greek god more than a real flesh and blood man.

I loved the show.

Yet I do have to admit with the night club pumping loud pop music, drunk people shouting instead of talking and my own superhero friends talking. I couldn't deny my head wasn't hurting.

It was pounding.

And my sense of smell was plain awful, as all the different hints of gin, beer and other alcohol all mixed together to create something flat out strange. I didn't know if I would stay here too much longer without being sick.

The sound of my friends laughing made me smile as I looked at two other superheroes from the same sector as me. Aiden was a really cute young man dressed in a hot white shirt, tight black trousers and some very stylish shoes.

Then his boyfriend Jack was another adorable guy who was basically wearing the same as Aiden just in a different colour shirt.

I always found it amazing how gays always managed to dress better than me in my jeans, pink shirt and blue hair. Granted I changed my hair colour like the calendar changed days, but I needed a hobby according to my friends.

So I choose dying my hair.

As superheroes in the counselling and therapy sector, it was normally our job to look after people, watch out for people in need and manage their mental health. But tonight was something very special because Aiden had just started working at my practice and I loved it.

It was so nice having another guy around besides Jack because my male clients prefer talking about their difficulties with a man instead of me as a wonderfully hot woman.

Relax, I'm quoting some of my clients. I'm not that vain. Ha!

"He's hot," Jack said pointing behind me.

I looked at the guy and it was the exact same guy who I influenced to take his shirt off, and him and his female date were really getting it on over there.

I really wished I could see what the woman was thinking about, feeling and experiencing.

Images of the woman killing, eating and frying the man entered my mind.

"Shit!" I shouted. "Fucking hell!"

Jack and Aiden just looked at me, so I quickly told them what I had seen and despite how drunk they were. They also tapped into the hot guy's and his date's minds and saw what I did.

"Hot guy's also thinking the same," Jack said. "Just not as fucking twisted,"

I quickly realised that the two killers or twisted lovers must have been groaning or talking or moaning to each other, because unless we're touching someone it's the only way how we can read their minds.

I really did love that about being a superhero, all the myths about therapists became true. I really could analyse people by how they spoke.

"What we do?" Aiden asked, clearly drunk.

I just smiled. "Well we are here to celebrate you joining my practice,"

Jack smiled too. He knew exactly how my mind worked sometimes and sometimes I could be a tat twisted myself. Just not quite as much as Jack, and definitely not as much as these two lovers.

"Want to implant some suggestions for tomorrow?" Jack asked.

"Of course," I said almost laughing.

I focused my influencing superpowers on the woman and made her want to be sick all over the man.

She suddenly vomited. All into the guy's mouth, over his stomach and all over his crotch.

Jack started laughing. I did too.

The man vomited too. All into the woman's mouth and into her hair.

They both looked fuming.

We were all laughing so hard no sound was coming out.

After barely managing to recover from laughing, I focused my influencing superpower on making the woman want to get out of there and not kill anyone tonight.

She didn't seem like she wanted to do that. She was fighting me.

I clicked my fingers and I felt Jack and Aiden lend me some of their superpowers so I could strengthen my command.

After a few moments I felt the command sink in and then I did the same to the hot man. He was a lot easier to convince.

But they both muttered something about other victims, and how much of a shame it was that they weren't going to be able to add to their tally tonight.

"There are a lot more vics out there," I said.

Jack nodded and looked like he was focusing on the man.

"Got it. All his victims are buried in his back garden," Jack said.

I focused on the woman and as she was talking to herself, I easily got into her mind and saw where she had buried her victims.

"Got it," I said smiling.

Jack hugged Aiden and they both looked at me.

"Should we really celebrate tonight?" Jack asked.

I just laughed at what he was referring to, so I focused as the twisted man and woman started to walk away, I really focused on them. I wanted them to feel extremely guilty about all the killing they had done and whenever that happened they wanted to confess to everyone around them.

They were already hesitant about that command.

I clicked my fingers, and both Jack and Aiden threw all their energy at me. I loved the feeling of their power, youthfulness and love flow through me.

Neither one of us wanted these monsters to hurt anyone.

The command went through and as me, Jack and Aiden just wet ourselves laughing as we watched those monsters break down in tears and wail, cry and shout about the killing they had done.

It was a hell of a way to end tonight.

***

About an hour later the night club was a lot more empty, the music, talking and shouting was quieter and the police had arrived. Me and Jack and Aiden had loved influencing the twisted lovers into confessing to the police, and thankfully they were never going to be hurting anyone ever again.

That damn well felt amazing.

And with the twisted lovers confessing about the other murders too, I just knew that all the other families of the victims were finally going to get justice, and that really was the perfect way to wrap up tonight.

All three of us got up and as I helped Jack carry a very drunk Aiden out of the nightclub, I just smiled at Jack as I felt all of Aiden's horniness just radiate from him. Whatever was going to happen when Jack and Aiden got home it was going to be good.

I was almost jealous.

Yet as we walked out on the cobblestone high street and I heard the police cars drive away. I knew we had all done an amazing thing tonight, and that was just perfect.

A perfect way to celebrate Aiden's new beginning at my practice.

Maybe this was definitely a start to something great, fruitful and exciting.

Actually, that was more of a definite than a maybe. And I loved it.

PART TWO: THE CREEPER INCIDENT

THE ROGUE GOD

CHAPTER 5

I fully admit that having to go and get milk is definitely one of the most mundane tasks I do, but there is a very, very particular reason why I do it.

Of course I could send one of my staff off to get such items, I could easily just teleport there or I could do what most people do in this day and age, I could just order it online.

My name is Matilda Plum, a superhero in the Counselling and Therapy Sector, so for me these little jobs like getting milk are just another chance for me to help people. It gets me away from my practice and out onto the amazing streets of Canterbury, England so if anyone is in trouble then I can find them, help them and improve their lives.

Well that's the hope at least.

With my practice being just off the high street with that delightful cobblestone path, tons of university students talking, laughing and musicians playing in the background, normally I would go to a shop for milk on the high street.

But today I wanted to change things up so I was walking along a little street with small well-kept houses lining the entire street, plenty of cars were parked which was normally considering it was the start of a Bank Holiday as it was May Day. Plenty of people had the day off and I had no doubt people would be celebrating their day off later on.

Granted most people would be going to the mini-May Day festival in the high street, I had already noticed tons of stalls setting up with games for the children. I had even helped a very stressed out manager calm down about the event, and I made him realise everything was going to be okay.

It was actually a rather perfect morning, not too hot, not too cold and thankfully not a rain cloud in sight. Which for England was probably as strange as it could get and there wasn't another person out on the street, so it was relatively silent.

And considering I spent most of my days listening and helping people with their difficulties and their conditions, I had always learnt to love the quiet times in my life.

"She's banging," I heard someone say.

Now if I wasn't the only person on the entire street then I wouldn't have been quite as disturbed as I was. But I looked around again and I was the only person out here.

Then I realised that my superpowers had picked up someone saying that, or thinking that, towards another person. And if my superpowers were getting concerned about what that person had said then I needed to check it out.

Thankfully I knew my two staff members, Aiden and Jack, at my practice, also superheroes, wouldn't mind a lack of milk for a little while.

I crossed the road as I felt my superpowers were drawing me towards the high street once again and that was strange in itself. The festivals didn't start until later on, barely any of the shops were open and no students had lectures. So there was basically no reason for people to be going to the high street this early.

A few minutes later I got very close to the high street when I noticed a very tall man wearing a long black trench coat, a cowboy hat and boots just standing in the alley I was going along.

I could smell how disgusting he was from here, I doubted he had showered in weeks or months or even years.

Yet that wasn't what got my superpowers so annoyed. I just got the sense from him that he was up to no good and that something strange was going on.

So I walked up to him. "Hi there,"

The man huffed and looked furious to see me. Then he looked me up and down and smiled.

Normally I'm used to this sort of thing because I am sort of rather attractive according to most people with my very thin, but healthy looking, body, my long hair that I had decided to dye a very light blue today, and my small breasts were apparently something people liked.

I felt something try to press into my mind.

I tapped into my shielding superpowers that stopped other people from tapping into my mind, and I tapped into his own mind to see what the hell he was doing.

One of the great benefits of being a superhero in the Counselling and Therapy Sector was the myths about psychologists and therapists were actually true now. So I really could analyse people by what they were saying and their body language and more.

I was flat out disgusted.

This man was such a creep. It seemed like he wasn't a superhero but he had a mind reading ability and he always focused on their sex lives.

The weirder the better for him.

Then instead of watching pornography at home, he would walk the streets reading the minds of people's sex lives and then he would "deal" with those images later on in an alley. Which was probably what I just stopped him from doing.

But perhaps the most annoying thing about his mind reading ability was how powerful it was. I was almost struggling to maintain my mental shield around my own thoughts, he was really interested in what a girl like me did in the bedroom.

"Stop!" I shouted into his mind.

The man fell to the ground, holding his head.

I really did love my influencing superpower, I

hated using it but I did love it when I needed to use it.

The man just looked up at me. It was only then that I realised he was nowhere as young as I believed, he wasn't university age in the slightest. He was at least thirty.

"Why are you doing this?" I asked.

The man just smiled. "It's hot. You clearly have some power yourself,"

That really made me curious because I had never met a person who wasn't a superhero with powers. It was strange but there was a minor possibility that this man was a superhero he just didn't realise it yet.

And no one from the superhero world had contacted him and recruited him.

I know from personal experience how difficult it was learning what I was, how to use my powers and what on earth was happening to me. To say it was a confusing time is a massive, massive understatement.

I was definitely going to need some help.

CHAPTER 6

"Natalia need a little help!" I shouted.

Moments later the entire high street fell silent, the creep froze in time and the most stunning woman I had ever seen appeared. As a woman who was very much drawn to both men and women, I cannot deny how stunning Natalia, Goddess of counselling and therapy and psychology was.

I flat out loved her long golden hair, amazingly fit body and her face was so model-like. No wonder she was a goddess.

Even though I had called Natalia twice before in my superhero career, I was still utterly shocked that I was going to be talking to one of the most powerful people in the world.

Power just radiated off her, and it was scary. I doubted I would ever get used to it.

Granted I mentioned the creep and the rest of the high street was frozen in time, it was more like Natalia had slipped us in-between instances of time so it just gave the illusion of time freezing.

"You called Matilda," she said.

I pointed towards the creep. "Seems he has some kind of mind reading power and he uses it to watch the sex lives of everyone walking past,"

Natalia frowned a little. "Have you got a cause or series of causes?"

As much as I wanted to say that I had, I had been too disturbed by his mind to study and analyse him in any great depth. His mind was just so wrong, creepy and twisted that I really didn't want to tap into it for too long.

But I had to.

I focused on the creep and really started to analyse his mind and then I relayed what I found to Natalia.

"His name is James Peabody, married with a wife and two kids. He used to be… a psychology student then he graduated and he couldn't hold down a therapist job because of his sexual appetite,"

How I didn't vomit I didn't know. It seemed like this guy was completely obsessed with having sex, watching porn and just masturbating.

"He wants to stop but he loves it too much," I said as I pulled out of his mind.

Natalia folded her arms and focused on him.

"Is he one of ours?"

Natalia laughed at me. And it really didn't feel good having one of the most powerful Goddesses and Gods in the entire world laugh at you.

"Relax Matilda. He actually is or was meant to be,"

I was just shocked. How the hell was this man meant to be a superhero working for us if he decided to abuse his superpowers like this.

"Remember Matilda. You were confused about your powers at first," Natalia said.

Damn it. I completely forget that Natalia could read my thoughts easily and analyse me.

"I think I need to plant the suggestion that he needs to come with me and stop reading people's minds," Natalia said.

Now I folded my arms.

"What?" Natalia asked.

"He has to be one of the most powerful superheroes I've met. Normally this sort of mind reading power takes a decade or two to develop, right?"

Natalia focused on the creep again and sort of shook her head.

"He is powerful. He could help a lot of people but he will need to focus," Natalia said.

Natalia clicked her fingers and the entire world and sound slammed back into me like a massive tidal wave for the senses. I almost jumped but I just focused on the creep.

"I'm meant to be a superhero then?" the creep said.

I could feel his mind reading ability just to take into Natalia's mind, and I stroked the surface of his own mind and I seriously wanted to vomit at the sexual fantasies he was dreaming of doing with Natalia.

He was just inappropriate.

Natalia grabbed him by the arm and she looked at me.

"Thank you for finding him," she said. "When I train him up, he could save and help and treat thousands of people, and that's all because of you,"

And with that they vanished.

CHAPTER 7

It turns out I might have completely misjudged the creep, because about an hour later as I was walking back to my practice with four pints of milk in my hand, I got a mental message from Natalia.

I was walking along a little off-shoot of the cobblestone high street with little old coffee shops and other wonders in Tudor-style houses lining the street. It was delightful with the hints of coffee, cream cakes and more exotic treats that I would have to try another time.

It turned out that Natalia was extremely impressed with how quickly the creep had been to train up. Before he fell into his sexual addiction he had been a great psychology student and junior therapist, and thankfully he had remembered most of it.

And I was surprisingly happy about that because it meant he could go out into the world, help people and improve their lives. That was never a bad thing.

I knew that Jack and Aiden would be wondering what took me so long, but they would be extremely happy that I helped someone and finally we could all have a nice cup of coffee together to celebrate.

Because the world always needed more superheroes, I was just amazed and grateful and relieved that I had managed to give the world another one.

PART THREE: THE TROUBLE STARTING

CHAPTER 8

I absolutely hate wolf whistlers. There is just no need for such outrageous behaviour and the people that do it are just complete and utter scum.

As I was walking along a delightful little path that ran through the massive campus at one of the local universities in Canterbury, England with large cherry blossoms in full bloom lining the path. All I could hear was the horrible sound of wolf whistling.

I had to get closer and teach the whistler a lesson.

My name is Matilda Plum, a superhero in the counselling and therapy sector, and it is my job to go round and see if people need any help, I solve their problems and I check on their mental health. But I do hate wolf-whistlers.

Thankfully I was walking with my best friend Aiden who was another superhero in the same Sector as me. But unlike my tennis shoes, jeans and a nice blouse, he was wearing some black trousers, a white shirt and black shoes.

He did look amazingly hot and sexy and now I really understood why his boyfriend Jack loved him so much. That was why we were walking through the university actually, because Jack wanted to see us.

As we kept walking through the path I noticed various women started to walk quicker when they passed a very young and tall man.

At first I was rather surprised that he was the whistler considering how handsome, attractive and slightly posh he looked, and I really liked his longish brown hair that was parted to the left. It was definitely smarter than my long hair that I had decided to dye a dark pink today.

With the sound of birds singing, students muttering how much they hated the whistler and the whistling itself getting louder and louder, I just looked at Aiden and he knew I wanted to do something.

Now one of the great things about being a superhero in the counselling and therapy sector was all the myths about psychologists and therapists were actually my superpowers. So people did need to watch what they say, how they acted and how they looked at me, because I could analyse them.

Both me and Aiden stood to one side of the path and tapped into our powers.

As I felt all the hate, anger and rage being directed at these women by the whistler I was just horrified. This man hated women with a passion, and he had… he had beaten so many up over the past few years and that only made him horny.

He always got off on beating up women.

I just looked at Aiden. He had actually gone slightly white.

"We have to stop him," I said.

Aiden nodded. "But there's more. He's part of an entire network of sexist pigs all around the world,"

I really didn't want to believe Aiden so I focused back on the whistler and really focused on him.

"Wow," I said.

I couldn't believe all this, there was actually a website in the dark web dedicated to the celebration, worship and sacrificing of so-called useless women. This Whistler seemed to be someone high-up in the website.

His name was Reuben Grant. I hated his name almost as much as I hated the man.

"We're going to need some more superhero and divine help," I said.

Aiden nodded and bit his lip. I just smiled, I too was rather excited about seeing and working with Jack and my other friends on this problem.

"I just want to deal with this man first," I said smiling.

Aiden started laughing as he could probably guess what I was going to do.

One of my favourite superpowers was the ability to influence people and make them do things they would never normally do, so I focused on the whistler and implanted three simple suggestions.

Firstly he would punch himself in the balls as hard as he could whenever he even thought about hurting anyone (regardless of what gender they were). Secondly, he would call the police and confess to all of his beatings and hate crimes. Thirdly, whenever he remembered and thought and considered his victims or hurting someone he would start crying like a baby too.

"Ouch!" the whistler shouted.

I looked over and laughed as I saw him fall to the ground crying like a baby and he kept screaming how badly his balls hurt.

A woman walked past.

He hit himself in the balls again.

I was laughing so hard I was struggling to breathe.

But me and Aiden had real problems to deal with.

We had to stop his sexist network forever.

CHAPTER 9

Before now I had no idea Aiden could teleport me and him back to my very large white office with its smooth walls, high-tech and expensive look.

A few seconds later jack appeared wearing the exact same as Aiden and the two men kissed each other quickly as I sat on my desk, and they sat on two modern chairs in front of me.

If we didn't have massive sexist problems then I probably would have opened a window or something because of how hot it was, but we had much bigger problems than the temperature.

Aiden quickly explained the situation to Jack including the name of the website and his face just dropped.

"The problem is the website is on the dark web," Jack said. "I was treating a guy once who was a depressed computer hacker, learnt tons and he said he liked to own me a favour,"

As much as I hated and refused to let our mental

health clients give us gifts, favours or anything else, I definitely felt the need to make an exception on this one occasion.

I just nodded at Jack. He went off and made a phone call.

"What did you want to do with all the members?" Aiden asked.

I grinned. "Well the police will deal with them legally. But I think we should do two things as psychologists,"

Aiden grinned too.

"I think we need to help the victims if any are still alive with their recovery, so they can seek professional help wherever they are in the world, know they do have a life after this and that they're free to live without fear,"

Aiden's grin deepened. "And the second thing?"

I just shrugged. "Let's give the world a major increase in the need for testicle doctors,"

Aiden just laughed. This was going to be amazing fun.

I heard our printer working and moments later Jack walked back in and gave me and Aiden pages upon pages of paper containing the names, addresses and bank account details of the members.

There were thousands.

I really didn't expect there to be so many sexist people spread all over the world.

"It will take us months to deal with all these people," Aiden said.

I looked up at the ceiling. "Natalia a little help!"

Natalia was my boss and Goddess of the counselling, therapy and psychology sector. If anyone could help us, it would be her and considering she was one of the most beautiful women I had ever seen, it was hardly ever a bad thing to see her.

A few seconds later she appeared in my office with her long golden hair, amazingly fit body and just such a perfectly beautiful model-like face. It was no wonder why she was a goddess.

Before she could say anything I quickly explained to her the situation and I honestly couldn't get an emotional reading on her. Her face was like stone.

Now if I was talking to a God or superhero who worked in the gambling sector, then I would have been fine. But considering counselling superheroes and goddesses were some of the most expressive beings in the world, I knew she was furious.

"James!" Natalia shouted.

I was almost a bit surprised she was deciding to call in James Peabody, another superhero in our sector, because I hadn't seen him since I had found him being a creep with his mind reading abilities, but apparently he was a powerful superhero now.

Moments later he appeared and wow! I meant I was leant towards men and women, with men being my main preference, but bloody hell with James in his tight silver suit that left so little to the imagination, expensive haircut and his movie star smile. He had changed so much since I last saw him.

I thought I was about to orgasm. And if that happened I was fairly sure Jack and Aiden wouldn't be too far behind me.

Natalia quickly explained the situation to James and he had to sit down. All of us hated this network and we were determined to take them all down.

Now we had our superhero and a Goddess team. We were ready.

We just didn't know how to get to them all.

I couldn't teleport.

So the problems just kept coming.

CHAPTER 10

In actual fact it turned out I could teleport, I just needed to have someone actually tell me how, it was a lot easier than I ever could have imagined. Literally.

So as I imagined appearing in number 250 of my list of sexist pigs, I found myself in an awful hospital room with dirty white walls, a large damp hospital bed and a very overweight man laying there, his laptop was still turned-on on the little table next to him, and surprise, surprise he had been typing messages into the sexist network.

The sound of someone crying and wiping away tears made me look at a wooden chair next to the overweight man, and I gently smiled at the crying woman sitting there.

I instantly knew she was the wife of this pig and judging by how blackened and bruised and upset she was, I knew she had been abused terribly over the years.

Out of the 249 people I had dealt with, and

healed their families, she had to be the worst affected person.

I slowly went over to her and it was clear as day as she just presumed I had walked in through the door and not teleported in. The woman was wearing long sleeves and I could sense how badly she didn't want me to see the damage.

I tapped into my calming superpower and directed it at her. She seemed to relax instantly and she smiled, it was probably her first smile in years.

As much as I wanted to stick around and really help her, I didn't have the time. I still had another 800 names on my list that I needed to deal with as soon as possible.

I gently placed my hands on her shoulder and tapped into my influencing superpowers.

"Hi there Harper. I need you to do a few things for me, the moment I left this room you will not remember me being here but my suggestions will remain. Understand?"

She nodded. I hated having to influence people this much, as a psychologist it just felt so wrong, but there was no time.

"The moment I leave you will file for divorce, seek professional counselling and you will learn to live with your trauma, going on to live a full productive life,"

She smiled and nodded. I hugged her quickly.

Then I went over to her idiot husband and grabbed him by the ear. He hissed in pain but he was a bit unconscious because of the cancer meds he was on. Sadly he was going to survive though.

"You will let your wife divorce you. You will not resist. Whenever you think about harming another living thing you will hit yourself so hard in the balls you feel like they will break open. You will feel so guilty for the rest of your life about your crimes and abuse that you will cry yourself to sleep every night. Do you understand?"

He slowly nodded.

I wished he would kill himself but my superpowers always added in the command never to kill himself or others. And I liked that.

"Last thing, you will call the police the moment I leave and you will confess to all your crimes. Understand?"

He frowned but nodded and he was starting to wake up.

With that little pig dealt with I just smiled, I had a lot more people to help and I was really looking forward to it.

THE ROGUE GOD

CHAPTER 11

About two days later me, Jack and Aiden all appeared back in my office at the same time and they looked exhausted. I couldn't blame them, I felt like I could sleep for decades.

I never knew teleporting, influencing and helping so many people could be so tiring, so as me, Jack and Aiden sort of moved the chairs in my office and half-sat, half-fell onto the warm carpet of my office floor. We all just smiled.

Each of us had helped about a thousand people in the past two, three days and it felt amazing.

The smell of intense coffee filled the office as Natalia and James teleported in, massive smiles filling their faces and plenty of cups of coffee in their hands.

But what surprised me even more was Natalia just sat on the floor as well. Let me repeat, a goddess sat on my dirty floor! I didn't know whether to be embarrassed, grateful or something else entirely.

Yet all five of us seemed perfectly happy as we

sat on the ground, smiling and just so pleased with what we accomplished today. Without me and Aiden discovering what had happened, and then the others helping us, I would hate to imagine how many more women would have been beaten and killed.

But thankfully that was never going to happen again.

Natalia clicked her fingers. "I forgot to mention everyone. I got a call from Hippocrates, God of Medicine, Doctors and Biology. He wanted to know why so many of his superheroes were having to treat swollen testicles,"

We all bursted out laughing and I was flat out pleased with all of us.

So as we all just laid there rolling around on the floor of my office laughing more and more about everything, I just knew that I really did have the best possible friends imaginable.

And there was absolutely no group of people I would rather have helping me treat, protect and help people.

No one else at all.

PART FOUR:
A TRUST SITATION

THE ROGUE GOD

CHAPTER 12

I have always been a rather trusting person, my parents used to say I trusted far too easily and I would probably be kidnapped sooner or later, not that they would care too much, but thankfully I wasn't.

To me trust is something so vital, precious and critical to everyday life that I always encourage and want people to trust me. And when I see people who can't easily trust others I always want to help them.

You could probably call it a compulsion in a way.

My name is Matilda Plum, a superhero in the counselling, therapy and psychology sector so I travel around helping people, improving lives and making sure everyone's mental health is positive.

And that's why I care so much about trust, because as a superhero psychologist and therapist, I need people to trust me so I can help them with what they need. Thankfully I have a superpower that helps people trust me, but I'm so naturally good at what I do, I rarely need to use that superpower.

I'm really grateful people trust me enough for that.

As it was a Saturday morning on a hot summer day with the air definitely feeling warm, but not too hot nor cold, I was walking through towards Canterbury train station with its small brick station building and large archway you need to walk under to get to the ticket machines and by extension the platform.

Originally my plan was to travel up to London for the day, go to a psychology conference for the next week and see who I can help in the evenings, but I just had that feeling that my plans weren't going to go quite as easy as that.

The air smelt wonderful with hints of bitter coffee, sugary doughnuts with a subtle hint of petrol from nearby cars. It actually wasn't a bad smell and it only made me more excited about my day ahead, but I could feel that something was slightly wrong with the air.

Normally when people are in distress, experiencing psychological difficulties or entering danger, my superpowers immediately pull me in that direction. But this time I was sort of just left wondering what was going on.

I kept walking towards the train station, listening to the trains come and go from the station, people talking and panicking about missing their trains and a few trumpets playing wonderfully from nearby musicians.

It was when I got to the large archway of the train station when I sensed someone close to me was in distress, so I turned around and saw a very young woman standing about ten, twenty metres from me.

The woman was leaning against the train station and the wire fence that stopped people from climbing onto the railway (stupid people as I called them), she looked like she was trying to be invisible but she was clearly upset.

From what I could see, she didn't look homeless or broke or anything. She wore skin-tight jeans, a white blouse with some high heels. Personally I felt like she was given off more young office worker vibes than homeless or runaway woman.

Yet I could be wrong.

Of course I knew I had to go over and talk to her, try to help her and then get on my way to my conference. But in my tacky jeans, black t-shirt and with my dark, dark purple hair, I almost felt embarrassed to go and talk to her.

And for the record, these are my -just-travelling clothes, once I got to my hotel I would change into something more professional to go to the conference.

Thankfully as a superhero of the counselling, therapy and psychology sector, all the myths about psychologists were my superpowers, so all I needed to do was get her to talk to me and I could analyse everything that had happened to her.

I went over to her and smiled.

"You okay?" I asked.

She just turned away from me.

"You look a bit upset. Thought I would check in on you," I said.

She huffed.

In case she wasn't too trusting of strangers, which I could partly agree with and see the logic behind, I tapped into my trusting superpower and to my utter amazement it didn't work on her.

I focused all my strength on her, and my trusting superpower flat out failed.

Just in case it didn't work I blasted a very hot middle-aged man with my superpower as he walked by, he simply smiled and winked at me.

My power worked, but for some reason this young woman was impossible to get her to trust me. That had never ever happened before, so I was confused.

Without her talking to me, it was a lot harder to analyse and understand what she was experiencing, but not impossible. The only thing I could possibly think was the cause was this woman had had her trust broken so many times by so many different people. She refused to trust anyone.

And the only way how she could refuse my trusting superpower would be if her refusal to trust anyone was such a core part of herself that she was nothing without it.

This was breaking my heart that this young woman believed she had to do that. It was going to take so much therapy to help her overcome these trusting difficulties that I was really excited.

I really, really wanted to help her.

"Don't trust people do you?" I half-asked, half-said.

"Leave me alone," the young woman said as she stomped away.

I just smiled as she spoke to me and I finally understood what was going on, and I tapped into her mind.

It was actually a really sad story because everyone she held dear had betrayed her in one form or another. Her parents had promised her they would never cheat on each other, then this young woman, Leilani, had caught them both.

Then they both promised her and her brother that the divorce would be painless because they simply didn't love each other anymore and they had both accepted that. But because of the nature of divorces, despite the new No-Fault Law in the UK, the divorce had turned messy, horrid and even hostile.

And to top it all off, both her parents had partners that flat out hated Leilani and her brother. Her brother was only 12 years old and Leilani was 18, so she had to basically raise him with no help from her parents.

I just felt so sorry for the woman.

But I was also starting to understand what I needed to do to at least get Leilani talking to me, and hopefully I would be able to plant the suggestion that her and her family needed to get professional help together.

I could see in her mind how badly Leilani wanted everything to be okay, and she loved her mum and dad and brother more than anything else in the world.

So that's what I was going to do.

I had to make things right between the family.

And I knew that was going to be harder than I ever thought possible.

A damn slide harder.

CHAPTER 13

It turned out that Leilani's father and mother did not want to see me whatsoever at their very nice posh corporation offices (same job, different locations) as they both worked with very different insurance firms, so I decided that I was going to have to target one of them and go from there.

I had decided to "go after" Leilani's mother in a way because she was the person who had broken Leilani the most. She was the first person to betray her, break her trust and once she did it she kept doing it.

Thankfully it was hardly difficult to track her down to her favourite lunch spot in all of Canterbury, a very small, cozy and rather wonderful Italian café off the high street. I did enjoy its Italian music playing softly in the background, its cozy little booths and very fit Italian men and women walking around.

For the waiters and waitresses alone I might have to come back here a little more often.

I found Leilani's mother, a woman called Grace, sitting by herself in a booth at the far back of the café. The booth was well-maintained and Grace looked perfectly at home here with her blouse, trousers and high heels.

She looked just like her daughter in more ways than one.

"Grace?" I asked.

She frowned at me but I sat down opposite her. These booths did feel wonderfully soft, cool and relaxing. Yet another reason to return here.

"Who are you?" she asked.

"Matilda Plum," I said extending my hand.

Grace just frowned at me and took out her phone and just ignored me. She was completely rude, so I tapped into my analysis superpowers and I was really surprised at what I found.

I had been assuming that Grace was an awful cheater who didn't mind causing her children distress and putting them through a foul divorce. But it turned out that Grace was in a lot of emotional pain over the loss of her children hypothetically speaking.

Yet I knew exactly why Grace felt like her children were dead to her, because they refused to speak to her.

I couldn't blame them.

"Take it your personal life isn't going so well," I said, tapping into my trusting superpower.

Slowly Grace put her phone away and focused on me.

"How did you know?" she asked.

"I'm good at guessing," I said. "I know Leilani misses you and I'm sure if you just-"

She waved me silent and she winked at the very hot waiter who delivered her some lemonade then went away.

"I don't want to talk to my kids," Grace said. "I have a career and those kids messed it up enough for me with maternity leave,"

I almost wanted to point out how maternity leave had been over a decade ago and Grace seemed to be perfectly okay now, but I didn't. I had to get Grace to admit she wanted to see her kids.

"I know you don't mean that,"

Grace looked like she wanted to fight me but I knew she would crack sooner or later.

"You don't know me," she said, trying to be angry but failing.

"I know you didn't mean to put your kids through the horrible divorce. Tell me, are you still with your affairs?"

Grace just looked in horror at me, I was surprised I didn't need to use any superpowers to make her feel guilty, but there she was looking guilty and like she was about to cry.

I focused on her and made sure she didn't cry. I didn't want her in emotional pain, I just wanted her to acknowledge why this was so hard for Leilani.

"I will not talk to Leilani," Grace said, drinking her lemonade.

"Why?" I said, tapping into my rarely-used truth speaking ability so she couldn't lie to me.

She was really fighting me.

"My... boyfriend will hurt her,"

With that Grace finished her lemonade and ran out of the café, a minute later a very hot waiter walked over and made me pay the bill. I was happy too, just seeing this hot waiter so close was payment enough.

But now I needed to find out who her boyfriend was.

And why on earth he wanted to hurt Leilani.

CHAPTER 14

In all my decades as a superhero, I have never had to spend so much time replaying someone's mind in my head, and I had to admit Grace's mind was rather dull for the first few hours.

You see, once someone has spoken to me I always have access to their mind (or at least for 24 hours) so it was really easy to find out who Grace's boyfriend was.

"You there!" someone shouted.

I was leaning against the warm metal fence around a massive construction site with massive cranes moving about, people shouting and drilling, and needlessly to say this was an extremely busy construction site where accidents were just a moment of forgetfulness away.

The man walking towards me was a very tall man wearing worker's trousers, a high-vi jacket and a red hard hat. He was exactly the man I wanted to see, because this Leon Jackson was Grace's boyfriend.

"You cannot be here," he shouted.

I just smiled as I activated my superpowers and analysed him. He was about the same age as Grace, clearly loved her and... oh!

I had been expecting him to be abusive, horrible and foul who was demanding Grace never see her kids again. He had said that to her but the context was completely wrong.

Grace had told him about how foul her kids were in an effort to get him to stop asking her to meet them. This Leon really wanted to be part of the family with Leilani and her brother.

"Wait you don't want Grace to not see her kids," I said.

Leon just looked at me. "Of course not. And who the hell are you?"

As much as I wanted to just say *psychologist*, I really didn't want to give him or anyone else for that matter any more reasons to hate me and my profession than more than normal.

"I'm just curious about Leilani. Could you do something for her please?"

Leon folded his arms.

"Could you please pressure Grace into calling Leilani? Leilani really wants to hear from her mother and she wants an apology,"

For a moment there I was sure I would have to activate my influencing superpower to make him do it, but he nodded and smiled.

"Of course," Leon said, then he gestured me to

go away. "But please go, this is an active construction site. Don't want you getting hurt,"

As much as I didn't understand how I could get hurt leaning on a wire fence, I smiled, nodded and just walked away.

Hopefully everything was going to work out.

CHAPTER 15

As I walked back to Canterbury train station in the middle of the afternoon, the sun was making the orange bricks of the station glow slightly, the air was crisp and cool and the only sound around the station was the calm noise of trains coming and going.

I was about to walk under the archway into the station when I noticed Leilani in the same clothes as earlier was still standing in the corner next to the wire fence. Yet this time she was on the phone to someone and smiling.

Really smiling.

The smell of burnt coffee, someone's aftershave with hints of petrol burning made me smile as I focused on Leilani.

It turned out that her mother had called her like Leon had said, he had probably called her the moment I left and now Leilani and her mother were finally talking again. They were laughing, smiling and it looked like Leilani was really enjoying herself.

I analysed her a bit more and I was right, and I was really, really happy that she was starting to trust a tat more. Sure she still had a massive wall around her emotions, but there was a tiny crack in that wall.

So I focused on trusting superpowers on her and when I felt them catch a little on her mind, I gently implanted the suggestion that she should get some professional help. Then because I'm a great boss I implanted the phone number of another superhero who worked for me called Aiden in her mind. At least she could contact him as soon as possible.

Because as I pulled out of her mind, I really knew that in her current state all her friendships, sexual relationships and her life would fail in the end. All because she didn't allowed herself to trust anyone, I didn't want that for her.

As I went into the train station and boarded my train to London, I couldn't be more pleased about helping that poor woman, and now she could finally start to get her life back on track.

And that was really was an amazing feeling, because once trust is broken, it has to be repaired. I certainly understand that a lot more after this case.

PART FIVE: THE CONFLICT IN THE SUGGESTIONS

THE ROGUE GOD

CHAPTER 16

On the whole I think it is fairly safe to say that humans are very suggestible people. From the media to politics to the choices of clothes we choose to wear, everything is designed to influence and suggest choices to us.

Now this isn't always a bad thing, suggestions about healthy food, better lifestyles and ways to improve our mental health are never bad things. And that is where I come in.

My name is Matilda Plum, a superhero in the counselling, therapy and psychology sector, and my job is very enjoyable and I really do love it. I get to go round helping people, improving lives and making sure their mental health is okay.

Suggestions can be a large part of my work (Ha. It seems cruel to call what I do work. I love it so much.) because a very large part of therapy is about suggesting and helping people to decrease their distress and improve their lives.

But this isn't exactly how my perfectly planned Wednesday afternoon was going to turn out.

You see I was in my "therapist room" (I only call

it that because apparently I cannot have two offices. Stupid rules) which was a wonderfully large room with white walls, colourful real art (not that modern art crap) and a wide range of comfortable chairs scattered about. Since I find that different people prefer different chairs, and so do I depending on the person or client I'm helping.

If I'm helping a child, they tend to love beanbag chairs which I have in the corner. Some adults love my surprisingly comfortable wooden chairs. And some teenagers... well teenagers are a very mixed bag.

So my plan for the afternoon was to have a two hour session with a brand new client who wouldn't tell me what difficulties he was having over the phone, so I booked a two hour session as I felt there would be a lot more to work through in the first session than I thought.

Then I planned to spend the rest of the afternoon doing some paperwork before I went out with some superhero friends from different sectors.

But the closer it got to my two hour appointment the more and more my awareness superpower, or spidey sense as others called it, was telling me something was very, very wrong.

I decided to check my therapist room, but everything was as it should be and the last hints of lavender, jasmine and soothing orange was going. It was one of my favourite smells but new clients had rather firmly told me they didn't always like it. But other clients loved it. That was just weird sometimes.

I also went over to my glass door in case my two other counselling superhero employees were in trouble. But nope. I could clearly hear Jack and Aiden in their rooms helping their own clients, they were okay.

Nothing seemed to be wrong.

I was just about to go over to my desk when there was a very loud knock at the door. I have never understood why people feel the need to slam and knock and bash on my door, but I suppose it's a small problem in the grand scheme of things.

When I opened the door and let in my two hour appointment, I couldn't help but focus on him. He wasn't a very attractive man per se but I just felt the need to focus on him. Normally I only studied a man or woman like this if they were hot but this man was not.

I carefully let him in, choose a seat and he laughed to himself and muttered something about this being a likely test. It wasn't. But still I just focused on him in his black jeans, long blue shirt and brown shoes. He clearly worked somewhere where he had to look professional, but I still didn't know why I had to keep looking at him.

We both introduced ourselves as he sat on a very comfortable but hard wooden chair. I did the same and was surprised he was called Richard Baker, he looked more like a Donald to me, but that didn't matter.

Since he had spoken to me I tapped into my analysis superpowers (the benefits of being a superhero psychologist) and got to see he was very disturbed about night time.

It seems when it got dark he would cry himself to sleep, whenever he thought about cooking a chicken dinner he would hit himself in the balls and he would just start confessing his love for his wife whenever someone mentioned love.

Now I was curious.

Because to me these all sounded like suggestions implanted in his mind by a superhero. You see when us superheroes depending on the sector, come into contact with a disgusting person who does horrific things we like to... make sure we use our superpowers for good. Making sure the idiots we deal with never do it again.

"Tell me Mr Baker, why do you think you keep hitting yourself and crying?" I asked.

For a few moments he looked terrified that I actually knew what was going on, then he smiled and just thought I knew because I was a psychologist.

It was because I was a superhero one, but that wasn't too important now.

Yet he just shrugged.

"I dunno know. Just kept doing it ever since I found a website,"

It would be quicker for me to search his mind but I wanted to hear him tell me.

"What website?"

He looked around. "Is everything I say confidential?"

I nodded. I had already explained that to him in our introductions but I could sense how embarrassed, frustrated and just annoyed he was acting like this. If he was a normal client I would gently help him to realise it was okay to be acting like this as I got him to understand there were better ways to behave and cope with life.

But he was far from a normal client. He was a possibly foul person, well he had to be for a superhero to implant these suggestions into his mind.

"What website did you look at?" I asked.

Richard looked at the floor. "A sexist one. A Wife beater one. A really bad one,"

I leant closer. I shouldn't have but again he wasn't a normal client, especially as me and my superhero friends had had to deal with a similar website a few weeks earlier.

We had targeted the website because of all the sexist pigs who were beating their wives and killing innocent women.

There was a chance this was one of those beaters.

"I only looked for a few minutes. I responded to some comments, I…"

"You were supporting their beatings," I said, impressed there wasn't a hint of judgement in my voice.

Richard nodded. "I thought they were joking. I thought the picture of dead women were… jokes,"

It took all my superhero effort not to judge him, hit him or deal with him.

He punched himself in the balls.

And when I tapped into his mind, I was surprised to see he hadn't wanted to hurt me, which we all agreed was the standard command we would give those horrible men. So why was this man punching himself in the balls if he didn't want to hurt me, a woman?

I looked up. "Natalia! James! Love birds!"

CHAPTER 17

A second later everything turned blurry for and then everything fell silent and Richard was frozen like a statue as Natalia, the Goddess of Counselling, Therapy and Psychology slipped us in-between moments of time.

As a woman who loved both women and men, seeing Natalia was always a special treat with her amazing golden dress, amazingly fit body and the sheer sexual power that radiated off her. She was stunning, but as she was a Goddess (no wonder) and my boss I was hardly even going to do anything.

Moments later James, Jack and Aiden, all superheroes in my sector teleported in all wearing smart suits, black shoes and golden watches, and as both Jack and Aiden looked worried I knew they must be at a critical moment in counselling their own clients.

Yet as they were boyfriends I quickly felt their worry run away.

"Why did you call us Matty dear?" Natalia asked.

I just pointed to Richard. "He was one of the targets on our hit list for the sexist website,"

James laughed. "Then he deserved what he got,"

I wanted to agree with him but I still wasn't so sure he was a guilty person.

"I don't think he was sexist and the idiot pigs like the rest of the targets," I said.

Natalia folded her arms. And when a Goddess folded her arms like that, I really wanted to run.

"What you want us to do?" Aiden asked.

"Does anyone recognise him from their list?" I asked.

Each of my friends looked at Richard intensely, and I was really glad he was frozen in time otherwise he might have died from a heart attack. Having three superheroes and a goddess stare at you wasn't exactly fun.

"Nope," they all said.

I paced around my therapist room for a moment.

"Wait," Natalia said. "No one here recognises him, but he was a user of the website,"

Jack stepped forward. "Remember we only targeted active users of the site. I doubt a person who used the site once would have been added to our list of targets,"

I nodded. I completely agreed and considering superheroes had amazingly good memories I believed that no one saw him.

Natalia focused on Richard and her stunning dark eyes glowed gold. Me, James and the love birds also focused on Richard.

A moment later I was coursing through his mind with the others and hundreds of mental images of memories flew past.

We were all looking for the very command that was making this poor man hurt himself for no reason.

It was so strange that a god, goddess or superhero would do such a thing.

The deeper and deeper we got into his mind the more I realised how innocent he actually was, and if his memories were correct (which I believed they were) I was impressed with how many sexist pigs he had punched in an effort to save women.

But his acts of heroism didn't stop there.

He defended blacks, gays and transpeople, even though his own opinion about transgender people wasn't completely made up yet. It was so interesting that Richard wanted to defend so many people despite the personal risk.

Then I slowed down inside Richard's mind and everything turned bright white. I clicked my fingers and the others appeared.

"What if this is about who Richard was before all this?" I asked.

Jack and Aiden looked at each other.

"Makes sense," Jack said. "Especially cos Aiden found a newer more powerful command that gives Richard an intense headache whenever he desires to help someone,"

Natalia frowned and our white surroundings dimmed slightly because of her rage.

"We need to find out who put the command in," Natalia said.

"Let's focus on removing it first," I said.

Everyone nodded and we went off coursing through Richard's mind again.

A few minutes later we found the commands in the deepest darkest depths of his mind. The commands were like a massive shadowy ball of oil that kept churning, splattering and tightening on itself like it was choking Richard inside out.

These commands were meant to kill him eventually.

The shadowy ball was inside an immense spherical chamber made from pure black evil with the walls having a slight shine to them.

"Do not touch anything," Natalia said firmly.

I wasn't going to argue.

"Everyone. Activate your suggestion superpowers," Natalia said.

Natalia's eyes glowed intense white as she focused on the shadowy balls, me, James and the love birds raised our arms and white light shot out.

Hissing filled the air as the white light coated and burned and killed the shadowy ball.

Then it started to grow bigger.

It was getting closer. I focused all my energy on my light. It got brighter.

The shadowy ball kept growing.

Natalia screamed in pain.

Us superheroes focused more.

The ball was slowing.

Aiden collapsed.

We focused more.

I screamed in agony.

The ball grew faster.

And faster.

It was so close.

James collapsed.

Jack collapsed.

Blood ran down Natalia's face.

I screamed.

I charged towards the shadowy ball.

Launching everything I had at it.

The ball shrieked.
It screamed.
It melted.
It disappeared.

Natalia slowly laughed before she collapsed and then I found myself still frozen in time back in my therapist room with three superheroes and a Goddess unconscious around me.

Something a very horny woman who just saved a man could definitely take advantage of.

But I won't.

CHAPTER 18

Thankfully it didn't take Natalia, James and Jack too long to recover, and it was great knowing they were okay. Then I simply tricked Richard into believing the two hours had flown by and he had had a blast with me.

He was always going to believe it but I did use my superpowers to make him really, really believe it.

It took Aiden a bit longer to recover but as all five of us sat on my wide range of chairs, I couldn't deny it was great to help someone with my favourite superheroes and Goddess.

But what really concerned me, I had dealt with rogue commands for decades back in the 1940s (yes I am that old. No I don't look over 30) and they never actively attacked you like that shadowy ball did.

Whoever had gone rogue and wanted to kill Richard was an extremely powerful and angry superhero or God.

"You still thinking about the ball," Jack said to me.

Aiden smiled and Jack playfully hit him.

I hadn't realised how deep in thought I was, but it was great smelling the hints of lavender, jasmine and soothing orange starting to fill my office again.

"I am," I said, "I just don't know who we're dealing with,"

Natalia kept frowning. "No offense. I do not believe a superhero did this,"

The rest of us could only nod. The idea of a God or Goddess going rogue like this was awful, it was rather impossible to think about. But the evidence was clear.

"Let me do some investigating and I'll be back in a few days, weeks or months. Well done all of you today. Especially you Matilda," Natalia said.

I just looked at her. "Be careful,"

She smiled at me and nodded. Then she just disappeared. Leaving my large therapist room feeling very quiet, empty and troubled.

Jack and Aiden stood up holding hands.

"Still on for drinks?" Jack asked me.

I had completely forgotten about me going out tonight, I still had my paperwork and admin to do, but after a day like this where I had saved an innocent person, found evidence of a rogue god or Goddess and almost lost my best friends. I could seriously use a drink.

So with James joining us too, all four of us quickly left my practice and went off to a local bar.

And after all the chaos from the past few hours, I just knew this was going to be a wonderful end to a very interesting day.

PART SIX:
THE MAGIC PROBLEM

CHAPTER 19

Human beings can think about some very, very weird things, but they can think about very normal things too. Some people think about sex a LOT (I like those people), other people think about their families, loved ones and jobs, then there are other people who think about weird things.

I don't really know what my weirdest find ever was, but I think it would have to be a young woman I came across a few years ago who wanted herself and her boyfriend to lose their virginity to each other, and wow. She had clearly watched way too much fantastical porn.

Thankfully I simply slipped in a few helpful tips for her and she… she certainly had a good night.

Oh yea, I should probably clarify. My name is Matilda Plum a superhero in the counselling, therapy and psychology sector. So quite often I have to slip into the minds of people helping them solve their problems, their psychological distress and improve their lives.

And I love it!

Today I was out with one of my best friends, a fellow superhero in the same sector (and my employee) Aiden as we went round a massive shopping centre walking on the top marble floor near some jewellery shops.

The shopping centre was easily the size of twenty football pitches with very posh shops, plenty of food courts and about every single shop a person could ask for.

The sound of people muttering, talking and complaining about how many people were here today echoed around the entire shopping centre. It was almost like all the sound rolled into one constant drone of sounds without even my superpower abilities able to pick out individual voices.

But I did enjoy the amazing smell of crispy fried chicken, succulent pork chops and spicy cheesy fries that flowed up from the food court below us. I was definitely going to have to steer Aiden in that direction later on, with the amazing taste of a fried chicken dinner forming on my very hungry tongue.

Granted it might have been extremely busy in here today but it wasn't too hot not cold. Thankfully the shopping centre had some killer air-conditioning that managed to help everyone stay cool, happy and kept them shopping.

Very clever.

Me and Aiden were walking past a very expensive

jewellery store with ten thousand pound necklaces, rings and bracelets firmly displayed on the outside enticing us to go inside.

Aiden looked like he was seriously considering something for himself or his boyfriend Jack. I was a little more cautious, because whilst both of us could easily afford to buy the entire shopping centre without any hint of bankruptcy. I just wasn't sure if the money was worth it.

Aiden went over to the store and focused on a very expensive rose gold bracelet with diamonds embedded into the metal. I have to admit it did look stunning, but seriously?

I was about to suggest we should move on in case we found someone who did need our help, but then I realised my spidey sense was going off.

I couldn't help but think someone in the store was in trouble, and judging by the massive smile on Aiden's face, he had sensed it too. Probably before me.

Then I noticed he wasn't actually looking at the bracelet he was looking past the window and into the store.

"Fine smartass," I said quietly to Aiden. "Pretend to be buying me the bracelet,"

Aiden laughed. "Pretend? I was gonna buy it for Jack,"

I almost threw up my arms up in the air. "Fine, buy it for me in the store. Then give it to Jack,

Aiden kissed me on the cheek. I quickly noted

down the item number or code was probably a more accurate way of putting it.

Me and Aiden went into the large oval jewellery store with a massive ring of glass cabinets lining the store and then there was another ring of counters in the middle. Everything looked so amazing, beautiful and stunning.

And I realised that Aiden in his black business suit, black shoes and perfectly styled hair was a lot more suited to this store than I was, in my far more casual jeans, a white blouse and dyed black hair.

There was a very fit six foot six man in a tight black waistcoat, trousers and smooth-shaven face that smiled at us, and me and Aiden almost raced over to see him.

He was the hottest looking man I had seen for ages and he was so young, probably 25, and wow… just wow he was hot.

"Hello I would like to buy item EQ24 for my lady please," Aiden said.

The man almost looked disappointed at Aiden, probably for acting straight. I just smiled.

"Of course Sir," the man said and gestured Aiden to go with him to get the item back out of the front display windows.

Whilst they were gone I really focused on the surroundings of the store, I had been so captured so that hot sexy man that I hadn't had a chance to focus on the other customers.

There weren't too many which made sense

considering the price of the store, but there were three other male staff members (that were equally hot as our server), a rich young couple with the husband holding a briefcase and a very non-rich couple.

I liked the non-rich couple because you could sort of tell that they only in here pretending to be rich, but they were so polite, kind and funny that I really liked that. And their server seemed to be fine.

That's why my spidey sense kicked into action and I focused on the man serving the non-rich couple. He was wearing the same waistcoat and trousers as our hot man, but he was slightly older (maybe 30) and there was just something wrong about him.

He still had beautiful eyes, and...

Come to think of it, I couldn't deny that everyone in this store was a little too attractive. Yea, it's normal for businesses to hire attractive staff members to help sales, but it is not normal for them to be attractive in the exact same ways.

Me and Aiden were talking years ago about our past boyfriends and there was never a repeat of what we found attractive about them. For example, my first ever boyfriend I liked because of his squarish face and white teeth. My next boyfriend I liked because of his funny attitudes and his smile. My last boyfriend (and yes of course there were men and women in-between) I found attractive because of his... wayward parts.

But everyone in this entire store was attractive because of their bodies, handsome faces and politeness. That wasn't natural.

So as Aiden came over to me looking worried, I knew he had figured out the same, and I tapped into my analysis superpower (the perks of being a superhero psychologist).

I found nothing.

It was almost like none of these people had minds at all. They didn't have any wants, memories or desires. It was so strange.

My spidey sense activated again and I focused on the rich couple. I analysed them and found they wanted to kill the non-rich couple for daring to insult their richness just because they were too stupid and poor to buy the things they could.

Aiden came close to me. "I think we need a bit of help,"

CHAPTER 20

"Natalia come out of time please!" I shouted.

A moment later the entire store went icy cold and blurry as Natalia, Goddess of counselling, therapy and psychology appeared next to me.

Everyone was completely frozen in-between the moments in time except me, Natalia and Aiden.

And even though I had worked with Natalia tons of times now, I still couldn't get over how stunningly beautiful she was with her long golden hair, amazingly fit body and her divine sexual power that radiated off her (or maybe that's just a fantasy of mine!).

Then I noticed how creepy, silent and awful being frozen in time was. It was so unnatural because there was no sound whatsoever despite the background noise being rather deafening only moments ago.

Natalia frowned at the three staff members. "Have you analysed them?"

Both and Aiden nodded.

Natalia stared at us and her eyes glowed bright gold. I felt her burrowed into the deepest darkest depths of my soul and it felt strange.

Then Natalia did the same to Aiden but more intensely.

"These people have come into contact with dark magic," Natalia said.

I gasped. I knew superheroes, Gods and Goddesses were real but I didn't know about magic.

I focused on the jewels and realised that all of them were just a bit too enticing.

"They must have used them on the jewels," I said.

Natalia nodded. "These people were fools. Using magic for self-fish reasons never ends well and now this people have probably infected others with the dark magic,"

Aiden shook his head and held his hand above the jewellery.

"I can sense the magic in the jewels. You think everyone who has ever bought them is in danger of becoming infected?" Aiden asked.

Natalia nodded.

I hated to think about all the thousands of people who could be infected with dark magic, and I hated even more to imagine how many might die from it.

Natalia extended her fingers towards all three of the staff members and the jewels in the store. She zapped them with her own superpowers.

"They're safe… but be ready to see what they

actually look like," Natalia said with an evil grin.

Me and Aiden nodded.

"I'll get the store's records and work with other Gods and superheroes in the other sectors to hunt down these jewels and destroy the dark magic,"

"Thank you," me and Aiden said.

Natalia disappeared and the sound slammed back into me.

And I was shocked at what I saw.

I was completely surprised to see the three staff members turn into elderly men with bald patches all over their heads, their suits were nothing more than rags and the jewels were clearly fake.

I just looked the hot man who served us.

"Shit," he said.

The sound of the non-rich couple laughing their heads off made me smile as at least someone was enjoying themselves. But I sensed the rage coming from the rich-couple, there was such hatred in their eyes that I had to act.

I focused on the woman of the rich couple. Aiden focused on the man. We burrowed into their minds using our influencing superpowers and I was going to make them regret thinking about them.

It was rather simple actually. I simply made them forget about wanting to kill the non-rich couple.

And I implanted a few suggestions to make sure this would never happen again.

I made sure whenever the woman thought about killing she would start crying like a baby. Whenever the woman wanted to judge someone because of their class or amount of money, she would slap herself across the face as hard as she could. And whenever she couldn't help herself to buying something nice, she would be compelled to buy the same item again and give it to someone less fortunate.

I pulled out of her mind and just started laughing. Aiden pulled out a few moments later and he fell onto the floor laughing.

The husband took his briefcase and swung it as hard as he could into his balls. He hissed and fell to the ground in agony.

The wife slapped herself across the face leaving a very bright red mark.

"I think our work is done," I said.

Aiden nodded. "Work? Don't you mean play?"

I just laughed at that.

Because he was absolutely right.

CHAPTER 21

After helping two depressed people at the shopping centre realise what was causing their depression and what to do about it, me and Aiden came back to my practice, told Jack about our adventure and now we were all sitting in my office.

I really did love the white bright walls, my very modern desk and how sweet smelling it all smelt, it was a very relaxing smell, and with no clients being in the practice it was perfectly silent.

It turned out Jack had held down the fort very well whilst we were out and he had helped a lot of people, which was just flat out brilliant news. I knew he was a great superhero.

A moment later everything went blurry for a moment and Natalia appeared. But she didn't look like her normal beautiful self, in fact she looked rather drained.

I offered her a seat and surprisingly enough she denied it.

"I came to inform you about our hunt," Natalia said.

"Did you find everything?" Jack asked.

Natalia frowned. "Negative. Or yes in a way. We found all two thousand jewels that contained the dark magic and stripped the magic out of the jewels, the owners and the homes they were in,"

I leant forward. "I sense there's a but,"

"I got my friend the God of Security, Magical Defences and Chastity, don't ask, to look at the case. And he found something very disturbing,"

As much as I wanted to know what the hell chastity had to do with magic and security, I felt like Natalia was a lot more disturbed than she was letting on.

"It seems like the three elderly men didn't just find the dark magic one day, and the dark magic corrupted them and their business. Someone infected them with the dark magic first,"

Me, Jack and Aiden just gasped. That was something beyond evil, it was one thing to become corrupted by dark magic. But for someone to willingly infect others, that was monstrous.

But I think I understood where she was going with this, there had been an incident only a few weeks ago about a rogue god infecting the mind of someone with mental commands that would kill them over time. That was a horrific thing to do.

And I had a terrible sense that this was another incident.

"The rogue god or goddess?" I asked.

Natalia slowly nodded.

Jack and Aiden looked furious and I didn't blame them. It was disgusting that a god would do such a terrible thing.

"I will keep investigating but I will get Gods and Goddesses that I trust involved because clearly this rogue is getting more and more dangerous,"

I nodded my thanks and Natalia disappeared.

All three of us just sort of sat in silence for a moment as the tension and reality of the situation sunk in. But there was really nothing more the three of us could do for a while, we were superhero psychologists, not detectives.

So finding this rogue god would certainly be a waiting game and tomorrow's problem.

And there was something a lot more important to do first.

I took Jack's and Aiden's hands and smiled.

"You know Jack, Aiden was going to buy you a very nice bracelet today, and because I helped him stop some dark magic from destroying lives. I think he should buy me one too," I said.

We all laughed at that and teleported off to another shopping centre to treat ourselves to some very nice jewellery.

Because we have the money, friendship and positive thoughts, and if you can't make use of them, then what's the point?

PART SEVEN: PRIDEFUL FUN

THE ROGUE GOD

CHAPTER 22

I had always flat out loved the annual Pride Festival in Canterbury England. I loved the happiness, colours and just how amazing everyone at the Pride event was. They were always so kind, generous and very protective of everyone else at the event, regardless of whether you were straight or gay or somewhere in-between.

But I still made sure I went every year, mainly because I always wanted to show my unwavering support for these people, and I was technically bisexual myself, but most importantly because I did it as part of my job.

You see my name is Matilda Plum, a superhero in the counselling, therapy and psychology sector. So these pride events are perfect for me since it is my job to travel around, help people solve their problems and protect their mental health.

Yet it is a very sad truth that pride events are almost like breeding grounds for my sort of help, but there are always people here who really want to experience their gay side but they feel extremely guilty because of their homophobic family. Other people simply need a little push in the right direction to feel at home here. And other people still are just conflicted about being so-called "normal" (whatever the fuck that means) and being who they really are.

As I started to walk down the wonderfully warm cobblestone high street with little shops lining the streets with their pride flags and special discounts because of the event.

I had already helped two young men who were on the verge of suicide, but I helped them to realise they weren't demonically possessed and that they were normal people that deserved happiness.

The sound of the music echoed all around canterbury as the event and parade and parties continued into the late afternoon. The amazing smell of cooking sausages, burgers and French fries filled the local parks and high street as everyone was looking forward to tonight's entertainment.

At these events I always made sure I bought the sexual essentials in case someone ever took an interest in me, and I was taught at a very early age (before I became a superhero actually) that if a good looking person wants to have sex with you. It was fairly rude to say no.

I stuck to the outside of the massive crowd of people as we all walked down the high street towards the massive park where the concerts, food and other activities were happening.

And then I noticed something.

Normally whenever someone was in trouble my superpowers would sort of pull me in that direction and that's what they were doing now. They were telling me to go away from the crowd and start walking back up the high street.

That alone was weird enough since everyone (and I really do mean everyone) was heading down the high street.

As I always refused to argue with my superpowers I started walking back up the high street, and saw my two employees and fellow superheroes in the same sector as me, Jack and Aiden.

I gestured them to walk with me and they did.

To be honest I was a bit surprised they looked as *straight* as they did. Both Jack and Aiden were wearing tight black jeans, blue shirts and blue trainers. But besides from that the two boyfriends only had a gay flag painted on their cheeks, compared to other people here today they really weren't making much of an effort.

At least they looked a bit more comfortable than me, I was really starting to regret wearing a white blouse, black trousers and high heels. It wasn't completely my fault as I did need to work in our mental health practice this morning to help some people. But these heels were killing me!

"Sense what we are?" Jack asked me.

I nodded. It must have been major if all three of

us were sensing it.

Then further up the high street I noticed that a woman was glowing slightly. I quickly realised she had a black aura around herself.

"Black aura," I said.

Me and Jack and Aiden quickly walked towards her, because a black aura only meant one thing. Death.

When we got to the woman she was rocking and bumping and crashing through the crowd towards us. But she wasn't making any sounds.

As superhero psychologists the three of us would be able to analyse her if she said anything. But she was clearly too drunk or high or something to do anything.

As she stumbled towards us, I had to admit she was beautiful. She clearly wasn't wearing a bra that I seriously didn't mind, her white shirt was soaked through and her jeans had clearly seen better days.

But why was she sweating?

The three of us quickly went over to her as she exited the crowd and fell on the ground.

Jack and Aiden grabbed her and pulled over and sat her down outside a nearby closed shop. The woman was sweating, crying and she was a mess.

But she was making a sound.

I concentrated all my strength on my analysing superpower and focused on what on was happening. I managed to get into her mind. And wow this woman was horny.

I had never been inside such a horny mind. She wanted to do everyone at the event, woman, man, transgender she wanted it all.

It was so hard to concentrate as her mind was getting more and more horny every second. It was like being drugged every second.

Maybe she was?

"What did you take?" I asked.

The woman smiled as her eyes went glassy.

Her aura went pitch black.

"We're losing her!" Aiden shouted.

Jack started to call the paramedics. Thankfully there were always paramedics nearby at these events.

I knelt down next to Aiden.

"What you got?" Aiden asked.

I shrugged. Focusing all of my superpowers on her. I really burrowed into her mind.

She was angry deep down. She had just split up from her boyfriend in London and she wanted to restart life. So she came down here and took some drugs.

They were drugs that her boyfriend had given her to help become more free. The bastard had drugged his own ex!

That was disgraceful.

"I need to see her ex. I'll be quick," I said.

The woman collapsed to the floor.

Aiden started CPR.

I had to hurry.

CHAPTER 23

I was going to make this bastard pay for hurting his ex-girlfriend. I quickly teleported to the address I had pulled out of the woman's mind and this was not what I was expecting.

Knowing how foul the boyfriend was from the woman's mind, I had been expecting a dirty apartment filled with weed smoke, drugs and just a disgusting apartment.

But that was far from the case as I appeared in a large perfectly clean apartment with a very white modern kitchen, the finest furniture and a very hot man staring at me.

Thankfully because of how my teleporting works the man would just assume I have always been in the apartment for at least a minute before I actually was. But wow, this man was hot in his fine Italian silk suit, gold watch and just... wow!

"What?" he asked.

I just closed my eyes and started humming a very

seductive tune and when I opened my eyes a second later. He was completely unconscious and I focused on what his mind had to tell me.

It wasn't hard to find the name of the drug he had given her, but he seriously loved her, he cared about her and it turned out she wasn't as bad in bed as the woman believed.

The benefits of being in two minds.

"Matilda!" Aiden shouted into my mind.

I had to return.

The woman was dying.

I had to save her.

CHAPTER 24

I quickly jumped back to the high street and the paramedics just nodded at me like I had always been there. I quickly told them the name of the drug and they looked a lot happier.

The paramedics pulled out something from their medical bags, injected her with it and the woman's black aura disappeared.

Me and Aiden and Jack all knew that the woman would be fine now that the black aura was gone, so the three of us gently used our superpowers to suggest the paramedics to leave. At least they would be free to help other people now.

The paramedics smiled, told the woman to go to hospital if she felt worse and they left.

The entire high street was a lot emptier now the vast majority of people had moved onto the park, and me and the love boyfriends looked at the woman as she slowly become more and more aware of her surroundings.

"My head's killing me," she said.

I laughed. "Yea. I'm guessing you overdosed on those pills your boyfriend gave you,"

I could sense her discomfort at me talking about him.

"He does love you. He really loves you," I said. "and you're actually a lot better in bed than you think according to him,"

A massive smile lit the woman's face. "Really?"

"Of course. He loved you so much that he was heartbroken about the idea of you dying. He wants to be with you forever," I said.

The woman slowly got up and her eyebrows rose. "How do you know?" she asked.

Me and Aiden and Jack all looked at each other and smiled.

"We're psychologists," we all said.

The woman quickly nodded like we were amazing all-known people because of our jobs then she quickly ran away in case we analysed her anymore.

Some of the myths people believe about us is just amazing.

I wrapped my arms around Jack's and Aiden's, and we all started to walk back down the high street, because after saving a woman's life I definitely needed some Pride fun.

Meaning dancing, eating and most importantly being around people that loved you.

And that really did sound like the perfect evening to me.

PART EIGHT: REVELATION

THE ROGUE GOD

CHAPTER 25

After living for so, so long I find it extremely hard to remember when I was actually born, before I remember running messages across the frontlines on my motorbike during the Great War so it was definitely before then. Then I was alive in world war two and I am still now.

So needless to say I know lost. I have no family still alive, no friends from my childhood and during those two wars alone I had lost more people than I ever thought possible.

Sure it was damn right impossible to deal with some deaths. Like the death of my family when the Nazis bombed our family home, deaths like the murder of my first ever proper boyfriend and girlfriend, and the list just goes on and on and on.

Death is just a part of life.

And of course that might sound extremely harsh, but after you've lived for over a century or more you learn ways to help yourself through the inevitably harsh times when someone you loved dies.

You see I can live forever (at least biologically speaking) because my name is Matilda Plum, a superhero in the counselling, therapy and psychology sector. Meaning it is my job (and utter passion) to help people solve their difficulties, improve their lives and maintain their mental health.

And death comes in a lot in my psychology practice in Canterbury, England. Most of the time when it comes to death, I tend to see people who are in deep down depression because of someone they love died.

But not always.

I sometimes have the amazingly fun job of travelling up to some of the UK's most secure prisons and talking to psychopaths, serial killers and other foul people thanks to my superhero friends in the prison, justice and policing sector.

As I sat in my favourite hard wooden chair in my therapist room with its large white walls with tasteful colour art hanging on them (none of that modern art crap was allowed), and my wide range of chairs for people to enjoy, I was starting to look forward to my next appointment.

The really interesting thing about this particular appointment was she had specifically requested the smell of lavender, grapefruit and passionfruit to be in the office for when she came in.

Now I became a superhero funny enough on the day Hitler invaded Poland so I have been helping people with their mental health for over 80 years (bloody hell!) and I have never had a request like that.

"Miss Plum?" someone said, knocking on the door.

As much as I wanted to wait the extra five minutes until the woman's appointment actually began, so I could enjoy the amazing smell and the taste of passion fruit cheesecake it left on my tongue, I decided that I better help her as soon as possible.

I went to the door and welcomed in the client, explained how the therapy would work and the other legal things I needed to cover. But this woman seemed to already know it all.

It's not necessarily that's strange, but if this woman had been in therapy before then it was perfectly natural for her to know this. But my spidey sense was telling me it was something else.

The woman was rather attractive in a way and I really liked her long blond hair, well-fitting (and suggestive) purple dress and her purple high-heels. She looked great but she didn't look like she was here for a therapy session.

As I watched her tit-ass-about trying to choose a seat (I mean I have a wide range of different chairs to choose from but it isn't an exam. Just choose one!), I kept seeing her flick back at me. Almost like she wanted to know exactly where I was the entire time.

"Is everything okay?" I asked.

She smiled as she pulled over a large blue beanbag and sat on it. I did the same out of politeness more than anything else.

Once we were both sitting down and comfortable I was about to tap into my analysis superpower when I felt her trying to do the same to me.

This woman was a superhero or something.

But then why would this woman be trying to analyse me?

This wasn't normal, right or fair in the slightest.

CHAPTER 26

"Enough," I said calmly into her mind.

She frowned.

"Who are you?" I asked.

"Eris Junior," she said.

My eyes widened. That meant she was the daughter of the Greek God of Mischief and chaos. What the hell was she doing here?

I felt myself sink into the beanbag and my hands and feet became trapped inside. I couldn't move.

"What do you know about the Rogue God?" she asked.

I just shook my head. Me and my friends had been dealing with a Rogue God that was commanding people to hurt themselves and completely abusing the powers given to us, but I still had no idea what was going on.

My boss, Natalia was meant to be investigating since she was a Goddess herself, but I hadn't heard anything for ages. So it was slightly beyond strange that Eris Junior was asking.

"Why you want to know?" I asked.

Eris Junior grinned at me. I sank further into the beanbag.

"Stop that," I said firmly.

She kept smiling. I kept sinking. I tried to fight it.

I tapped into her mind. I commanded her to stop. She didn't listen.

I focused more and more. She still didn't listen. I sank faster and faster.

"Natalia!" I shouted.

Eris's eyes widened. She kept grinning. My boss didn't turn up.

That never happened. Normally whenever I shouted her name she came running to help me.

She wasn't here.

"I am a superhero of Mischief and chaos and confusion," Eris Junior said. "Your friends think they are with you, having dinner and talking with them. They don't know you are with me,"

My eyes widened. That was flat out impossible, I didn't want to know why Eris Junior had created a body double of me, but it was clearly real and I was in danger.

"Why?" I asked.

Eris stood up and wrapped her hands round my throat.

"I want to know about the Rogue God,"

I could only smile as she was touching me, my influencing and analysis superpowers worked in a lot of very fun ways. I could analyse someone if they were speaking or touching or merely looking at me. I was that good, and Eris Junior was that stupid.

Her mind was interesting and rather like a playground. But I knew her mind was more akin to a rose garden, something beautiful with deadly spikes, rather than a playground to read and study and enjoy.

Whoever had helped her out with all this mind work had clearly wanted me to read her mind probably and wanted me to mentally injure myself in the process.

I pulled straight out of her mind.

Yet that mindscaping and forcing her mind to work in such specific ways so that it would be dangerous for me took some extreme skill. Again, no superhero could do that sort of work, only a god or goddess could.

"Do you know who the Rogue God is?" Eris Junior asked. "I do,"

I seriously doubted that for some reason, after all she was a superhero of mischief.

"Do you want me to tell you?" she asked.

She whipped out a knife. Pressing it against my nose.

"I could tell you but then I'll have to kill you,"

She was bat crap crazy this woman!

Then I realised something very important about this entire thing.

"Wait, you have a body double of me," I said.

She took her hands off my throat, came in front

of me and nodded.

"And that would require a mental connection between me and the body double, correct?"

She frowned. I was right.

"You stupid idiot," I said. "You might be clever in your mischief but the mind and human behaviour is my domain,"

I closed my eyes and really focused on myself. I felt my superpowers coursing through my mind and I found it. I found a very large shadowy ball in my mind that was never meant to be there.

I had no doubt that shadowy ball was connected to the body double with my friends.

"Fuck you bitches!" I shouted into the shadowy ball. Hoping my body double would say that to my friends.

And the one thing I never did to my friends was insult them.

Eris Junior jumped me.

My hands and feet were still sunk in the bean bag. They couldn't move. Eris threw me to the ground.

My wrists and ankles snapped.

I screamed in agony.

Crippling pain filled me.

Eris Junior smashed her fists into me.

Again.

And again.

My nose broke.

Golden fire shot into Eris Junior.

Throwing her against the wall.

A few moments later a stunningly sexy woman with a long golden dress, golden glowing hair and the most beautiful face I have ever seen stepped over me. Natalia, Goddess of counselling, therapy and psychology blasted Eris Junior with another fireball.

My pain grew in intensity.

I collapsed into unconsciousness.

CHAPTER 27

A few hours later I woke up on my wonderfully soft and cool sofa in my therapist room staring up at my bright white ceiling. As much as I wanted to move I knew I couldn't just yet, I still felt a little weak after the attack.

Thankfully my wrists and ankles were perfectly healed, fixed and felt as good as new. Believe me, I was more than pleased about that and I just knew that Natalia was behind it.

The air smelt amazing of hints of mint, pine and other refreshing scents that I couldn't quite identify, I immediately knew why Eris Junior had requested the strange scents of lavender, grapefruit and passionfruit earlier. Because according to superhero folklore they increased the powers of mischief superheroes.

I doubted it, but maybe I should reconsider that opinion.

"You okay?" I heard a man say.

I slowly forced myself up and I sat carefully on

my sofa, and truly smiled as I saw my best friends were all around me. Natalia was still glowing and beautiful as always, then my fellow superheroes and employees Jack and Aiden were there too.

It was so, so good to see them.

"What happened?" I asked weakly.

Natalia smiled. "You swore at us. We knew something was wrong so I teleported here and found Eris,"

I only frowned at her name. "I think she's working with the Rogue God,"

Natalia nodded. "She has been imprisoned and interrogated for her crimes. She will never see the light of day again but I believe I am one step closer to finding out who is behind this,"

"Thank God… Goddess," I said.

We laughed and Natalia kissed me on the head (I absolutely loved her power, chemistry and electricity flow between us) then she disappeared.

Me, Jack and Aiden sat in silence as I just hated to imagine that this Rogue God now had superheroes being corrupted and falling to his side. I hated that idea.

Because Eris Junior had really proved a point in all honesty, she had clearly been struggling with herself, and that's why she had been so easy for a God to bend her to his will, since Eris Junior was really only a puppet.

I didn't know exactly whatever mindscaping or suggestions this Rogue God added to her, but I had a very good sense he had a few extra commands. Believe me no superhero would have attacked another without being commanded to.

It just wasn't how the world worked.

So I actually had little doubt that Eris Junior had died in some fashion, been replaced with an alternative one and that was the struggle we were all facing.

How the hell did a superhero fall to the evil of the Rogue God?

As much as I wanted to find out, that was certainly tomorrow's problem, so I simply got up and grabbed my two best friends.

"Fancy a real dinner with me?" I asked.

Jack smiled. "You gonna swear at us again?"

I just playfully hit them both as we teleported away. "You know I don't swear you little shits,"

CHAPTER 28

Weddings, love and marriages always have been rather strange to me. I've been in love tons of times but as most people know things don't always work out. I've also been married and had some weddings a few times, maybe five or six or even seven, but they all ended in similar ways. Divorce, murder and more death.

Now I understand if you think I'm some kind of cold psychopathic killer, but please relax, I am far, far from that.

You see my name is Matilda Plum, a superhero in the counselling, therapy and psychology sector. And I was most probably born in the 1890s or 1900s (it's hard to keep track when you're as old as I am) so there are plenty of chances to get married, fall in love and die.

And yes that order is very much correct, because back in the day you never married for love. And I should know my parents kept selling me and my siblings into marriages for ages, things kept happening to my husbands, but I heard most of my siblings learnt to fall in love with their husbands.

I'm more than happy that times have changed.

Anyway I'm standing next to a large apple tree on the grounds of the massive cathedral in Canterbury, England with its immense spires, large roman walls and gothic architecture that made it a perfect place for a wedding. Especially with the sun being perfectly warm and shining down upon a very happy couple.

I had no idea how the happy couple managed to get married in Canterbury Cathedral, besides the fact they must have had some killer connections, but they looked so perfect together.

The insanely hot man was wearing a tight waistcoat, trousers and silk shirt that made me feel like I was going to orgasm at any moment. He was that hot.

The equally stunning sexy wife looked so fit in her tight white wedding dress. And her hair... wow, her long brown hair was styled so perfectly that it only amplified the natural beauty of her face.

Both of them were so stunning that I would happily jump in there in a threesome if they requested it. And if I was an unethical superhero well... I do have an influencing superpower. Ha!

The air smelt so refreshing with hints of mint, pine and freshness that it really was the perfect day for a wedding. Especially with a very young man walking out wearing a very cute suit (this would turn into a foursome soon!) holding a very expensive camera. He was clearly the wedding photographer judging by how the couple were posing, but he was a tat young actually.

Then another person, a woman this time, came out and helped the photographer get ready. She was clearly a sister or something judging by the way the young man and woman were looking at each other. Half looking in love and respect, half looking in annoyance and frustration.

Then another woman of the same age came out of the cathedral and positioned the happy couple for the photo. She too was clearly a sister. Now this was slightly beyond me, three siblings all rather young and all helping the happy couple with their photographs.

Thankfully as a superhero psychologist all the myths, misconceptions and other rubbish I have to deal with normally, are now my superpowers so I can analyse them since they were talking to each other.

As I tapped into that superpower more and more I was completely shocked.

The woman was a serial killer who slaughtered her husbands in some… rather graphic fashions every year on the exact same date, granted there were sometimes a few weeks difference, but it was almost always about the same time.

Yet she couldn't remember how many people she had killed, what she had done with the bodies and if she enjoyed it or not.

I focused on the man and he was just as weird. He always killed his wives whenever the sex was lacking and he was… he was always going to kill them on the same exact day as the wife did. When these two actually got to killing each other that was going to be interesting.

But he also didn't know how many people he had killed, what he had done with the bodies and if he enjoyed it or not.

Neither one of them had a clue. It was flat out weird.

I needed help now!

CHAPTER 29

"Jack and Aiden!" I shouted.

The entire wedding party smiled and waved at me. I almost felt embarrassed then the world went blurry for a second and two men were standing next to me everything was okay.

Since the great thing about superheroes and Gods teleporting was we made sure everyone round us just thought the newly teleported person in was always there.

Aiden and Jack, my best friends and my employees as they were both superheroes in the same sector as me, folded their arms and just spat on the ground.

Normally people would imagine that was just flat out strange and disrespectful, but considering Aiden and Jack had been boyfriends for over a decade now, and both of them were even older than I was.

I had heard plenty of their stories from over the centuries where the religious leaders tortured them because they loved men, and it was unholy according to a two thousand year old text.

"Sorry guys. Wouldn't have bought you here if it

wasn't urgent," I said.

They both weakly smiled at me.

"Tap into their minds and tell me what you see," I said.

They both shrugged, probably expecting to see a normal happily wedded couple. Then their faces turned to sadness, shock and horror as they focused back on me.

When they told me what they saw I just nodded because they saw the exact same as me.

"It's weird about them not knowing about if they liked it or not," Jack said.

I completely agreed. "New plan. Let's completely focus on the bride. All three of us focusing on her should help clarify the situation,"

They nodded and we all focused our superpowers on the bride.

Now there were two other superheroes helping me, her mind was a lot easier to understand and there were so many levels here that it was fascinating to see.

Then I figured it out.

I directed the images I saw back to Aiden and Jack as I finished with them. It seemed there were never any real killings, murders or anything illegal, it was all make believe.

And the more and more I unpeeled the layers of this woman, the more passion I realised she felt towards the groom. Because he was always the same husband, she had married him when she was eighteen, they kept having sex then a year later they started arguing. A LOT.

So in one of their fights they both shouted about would the other one be sad if they died. Both said they would be heartbroken and completely lost without each other, because they truly, truly did love each other.

In the crazy end of this massive fight both of them faked their own deaths, move to another city and started the romance all over again.

They had done this eight times now.

And the three very, very young adults showing the photos were from their first marriage, but I was completely shocked at how close they all were.

The children of course found it was a little weird their parents kept doing this, but it only seemed to make the family stronger.

Me, Jack and Aiden pulled out of the wife and immediately searched the husband's mind. He only confirmed everything but my god was he horny.

I had never been inside such a horny man. All he wanted to do was rip off his wife's wedding dress and start the romance all over again until they died.

It was so strange!

After the three of us pulled out again, we all slowly started to walk away, down a little block-paved street towards the high street. We all sort of just walked in silence for a little while, just letting the craziness of it all sink in.

Then Jack kissed Aiden on the cheek. "I would want to make us work no matter what,"

Aiden really smiled at his boyfriend and kissed him.

"I do to. I just hope we never go to that extreme," he said.

The two lovebirds wrapped their arms round each other's waist as we walked and I realised they were completely right.

Sure the married couple definitely had the

craziest wedding I had ever come across, but it wasn't hurting anyone. Meaning it didn't fall under our job to interfere and help with, and I was fine with that.

In fact I was glad about it. I was really glad that those two (seriously hot) people had found a way to make their lives, love and romance work in a way that suited them.

I felt Aiden's and Jack's horniness radiate off them, and I just nodded to them.

They teleported away and I was pretty sure they were going to make their bed very, very messy this afternoon. And after being inside the groom's mind, I seriously understood that.

So I was definitely going to call a *special friend* of mine too, because isn't it only polite to make adult fun after attending a wedding?

I think so. And I sure as hell wasn't going to waste this excuse!

CHAPTER 30

If anything else I am far from a vengeful person, I really am. Even though I have been alive for hundreds of years I am very grateful that I have always been a calm, helpful and rather dynamic woman who can handle herself and never has to resort to violence.

And trust me when you've been living for as long as I have you always find yourself in some flat out weird situation. Like my favourite was when I was alive in the 1950s when homosexuality was still illegal in the UK. I was going about my business in London, took a few wrong turns and ended up in a lesbian sex club. It certainly wasn't the worse mistake I've ever made...

But I think what happened today was certainly going to challenge my commitment to nonviolence.

My name is Matilda Plum, a superhero in the counselling, therapy and psychology sector. So it makes complete sense that I don't hurt people because as a superhero psychologist my job (and passion) is simple. I go round helping people solve their problems, protect them and protect their mental health.

I didn't hurt them.

It was a wonderfully warm Friday lunchtime with the sun high in the sky and shining strongly through my massive floor-to-ceiling windows in my therapist room with its large bright white walls, wide range of chairs for clients to choose from and the most amazing smells of lavender filling the air. I really did flat out love the smell.

Everything about my therapist room was brilliant and I had always loved it ever since I opened the place with my now-two superhero best friends Jack and Aiden. I could hear them flirting and talking and laughing away in the reception area as the practice was closed for the afternoon, and soon all of us would head home.

Well, I wasn't. Because more than anything else in the entire world I seriously wanted to hunt down someone who me and my friends have been after for ages.

Me, Jack and Aiden were superhero psychologists so all the myths, misconceptions and other nonsense we have to deal with on a daily basis were our superpowers. Meaning we could thankfully analyse, influence and help people.

Yet for the past few months it turns out that a rogue god or goddess with similar powers had been influencing innocent people to hurt themselves and others. We were all outraged because it was unthinkable that a god would do such a horrific thing.

So whilst my boss Natalia, Goddess of counselling, therapy and psychology was investigating through her divine friends who it could be, I really wanted to investigate it as a superhero.

Two people knocked at my door and just came in without me even giving them permission.

I just smiled when I saw it was Jack and Aiden holding hands as they came in with massive smiles on their faces. They clearly hadn't changed into normal clothes yet which was what they normally did before they went home together.

They were both wearing a very smart and professional black silk suit, blue tie and they made such a cute couple. I still think I looked more casual and approachable in my tennis shoes, light blue trousers and light blouse. Yet I really wasn't too fussed with my dyed red hair today, I wasn't going to do that colour ever again.

"Where should we start?" Jack asked.

I smiled. It was great to know they wanted to help me find the Rogue God as we were calling it, especially as I sensed earlier that they had better more exciting plans for this afternoon.

"I…" I started before my spidey sense activated.

I went over to my massive window and looked up at the sky, there was a large and very low passenger plane flying with an extremely black aura around it.

Something very bad was about to happen.

THE ROGUE GOD

CHAPTER 31

I pointed to the plane. Jack and Aiden saw it. They nodded.

We teleported aboard.

Yet the weird thing was when we teleported to it, it was completely empty. There wasn't a single person in any of the rows, none of the oxygen masks were down and the even stranger thing was it looked like no one was ever on here in the first place.

The horrible smell of poorly recycled air filled the plane and it was good to know at least the oxygen system was working well. It was just so strange, where were all the people?

"Up here!" Aiden shouted near the cockpit.

Me and Jack teleported over.

In the tiny square metre piece of floor in front of the cockpit was a massive bomb.

I could see the cockpit was empty. The plane was on autopilot. It was flying straight towards a local university.

We had to stop this.

The bomb was buzzing.

I looked at Aiden. I looked at Jack. No one knew

how to diffuse a bomb.

The bomb glowed bright red.

I didn't know what to do. We were about to die. All those students were about to die.

The bomb hissed.

"Natalia help!" I shouted.

The entire world went blurry for a moment and then Natalia in her stunningly beautiful golden dress, long golden hair and amazing smile appeared. She just looked at the bomb as we were all in-between moments of time.

"I will have to use my powers to contain the blast," she said.

We nodded. But I made sure to take tons of photos of the plane and bomb on my phone first.

"Done?" Jack asked.

I nodded.

"Go!" Natalia shouted.

The three of us teleported off and reappeared in my therapist room.

A few moments later I sort of felt like the plane had disappeared from normal sight and now only us superheroes could see it.

Then it exploded. Shattering the plane.

Natalia appeared next to me. "I tried to contain it. It was too powerful and…"

I hated it when gods and such powerful beings trailed off like they were scared. Like what the hell could scare a god!

CHAPTER 32

Jack and Aiden wrapped their arms around me and took my phone. Aiden flicked through the photos until he found a very clear one of the bomb, both him and Jack sighed.

I had no clue why.

"This is Olympus technology," Aiden said.

Wow! I knew Jack and Aiden were slowly studying the history, lore and myths around the gods, Goddesses and superheroes. But to think that Mount Olympus was actually a real place was incredible.

Natalia stood so close to us that I could start to feel her sexy body heat.

"I think I know who is behind this, yet if that is true. Then this problem with the Rogue God has been decades in the making," Natalia said.

"How?" I asked.

Natalia just looked out the window. "Before Mount Olympus, Atlantis and the Greek Underworld was destroyed. They had so much technology that it makes your science fiction look primitive,"

My mouth dropped.

"We were masters of everything. We created

entire dimensions for fun, and when Ragnarök hit the Norse Gods fled into their own dimensions. That always happened to all Gods and Goddesses throughout time and space whenever their religions collapsed,"

This was just fascinating.

"This bomb we just stopped. It was relatively primitive even more when compared to Olympus technology," Natalia said. "Yet there is only one man who could have created it, and now we must see them,"

Natalia swirled her hand in the air and suddenly me, Jack and Aiden were standing out in some hot volcanic valley somewhere in Europe. The ground was completely made from sharp deadly volcanic rock, the valley below us looked like it would kill you in a moment and the sun just beamed down on us like it was going to melt us.

A moment later Natalia and two men appeared. For some reason I got the sudden urge to knee to these two men in their white robes and extremely fit bodies as I felt the sheer power radiate from them.

The two men clearly knew Natalia very well and they were completely ignoring us.

"Athena!" Natalia shouted.

A second later a very fit beautiful woman appeared with long brown hair wearing nothing but a long white robe that left little to the imagination. But considering Athena was the Goddess of war strategy I had no doubt that was on purpose.

"You have gone too far this time," Natalia said firmly.

Athena laughed. "I was only playing my dear. I was only suggesting, influencing and weaving fate to my tune,"

"That is not for you to decide," I said.

Natalia smiled. The other two men seemed shocked that I could speak.

"I am the Goddess of War Strategy, weaving and wisdom. It unwise for you to speak to me mortal,"

I spat at her. "You suggested a league of sexist pigs to create a website to celebrate the beating of women. You suggested an innocent man to hurt himself. You! You are a monster!"

Athena laughed hard. "It was always a strategy little human. My strategies are perfect. I wanted to get rid of the sexist pigs of the world so I created a trap for them. You fell into the trap and you ended the threat,"

My stomach tightened.

"I wanted to experiment with suggesting things to innocent people. I had fun. The man didn't die like I wanted to, but I still learnt a lot. My wisdom grew," Athena said.

"You tried to crash a plane into a university filled with students!" Jack shouted.

Athena grinned. "I needed the wisdom that came from that experiment to see if Olympus technology still worked. This was always about gathering wisdom for my war strategies,"

Natalia and the two men laughed hard.

"The war that ended Mount Olympus is over. There is no more war," one of the men said.

Athena shook her head like he was lying.

"Enough," Natalia said flicking out her hand.

Athena's mouth moved but no words came out.

Natalia and the two men thrusted out their hands and gold light shot out of them. Athena disappeared.

The two men turned to me, Jack and Aiden and bowed. Then they teleported away. Natalia flicked her wrist and we were all back in my therapist room.

I was flat out shocked at everything that had just happened. Natalia smiled and waved at me, I felt my legs get excited, then she just teleported off.

It was great to see jack and Aiden also looked shocked, but their shock looked like it had come from meeting legendary people that they only knew about. I had no clue who those people just were.

"Care to enlighten me?" I asked.

Jack took my hand. "Those two men were Zeus and Poseidon. Then them and Natalia just banished Athena to the new underworld where she will be imprisoned for the rest of time unable to leave for abusing her powers,"

Again my mouth dropped and I was amazed that I had just met the two most powerful gods in creation and I hadn't even known. This job was amazing!

But I was a lot more pleased about finally knowing who the Rogue God actually was, well it was actually a Rogue Goddess but I still felt wonderful. After having to deal with Athena's mess for so long, it felt so great to be able to put all that behind me.

And back before I became a superhero I always loved to do a very specific thing after a major victory. Especially after victories in the first and second world wars, I always loved to party (and have sex). Sure I couldn't have sex with Aiden and Jack (I was completely the wrong gender for them), but I could at least have a great party.

So as I told Jack and Aiden my idea and saw their faces lit up in excitement, I just smiled to myself because this was really the end of something great. At least now I no longer had to worry about some Rogue hurting innocent people, encouraging sexist pigs to beat up women and crash planes into universities.

It was all over.

And I didn't even need to resort to violence or vengeance or foul language like so many others would have done in my situation. That was a great feeling and one that I was really looking forward to rewarding with my best friends in the entire world.

CHAPTER 33

The wonderful, breath-taking, amazing smell of sausage rolls, rich chocolate and other desserts filled the air of my little therapist room as me and Aiden and Jack started celebrating our victory. The soothing sound of music playing from my phone hooked in with our speakers played softly in the background creating such a warming relaxing atmosphere.

It was great to see Aiden and Jack dancing together, laughing and kissing. They laughed at my dancing, but I think I was rather great, naturally.

Octavia turned up, kissed me and we danced together playfully to some silly pop music. Everyone laughed, congratulated and cheered each other for everything they had done, and even Natalia herself turned up and joined in the fun.

As the amazing afternoon party stretched into the evening and late into the night, I was truly grateful, surprised and honoured to have such great friends that actually wanted to be here with me.

As a superhero I got to help tons of people and I truly loved it, but it was always assuring and great to know that I had people who had my back and would happily support me.

I loved them, and they definitely loved me.

Later in the night as we sat on my wide range of chairs in various stages of drunkenness (I had no clue a Goddess could even get drunk), we all sort of just smiled at each other in silence with the music playing in the background. It wasn't a bored, awkward or strange silence. It was the type of silence that people occasionally just fell into because they were all so comfortable with each other.

This was the type of silence where people knew they didn't need to talk, dance or drink together to know they were perfect and intimate together.

And that was why I loved my friends, because they were true friends that I could rely on for anything, even taking down rogue goddesses.

At midnight Jack and Aiden teleported home, I had little doubt their bedsheets would be very messed up tonight. Then with the flick of a wrist Natalia was sober and she left me and Octavia together in my therapist room.

Octavia took one look at me and smiled and took off her little black dress. And well, the rest of the night was only just beginning.

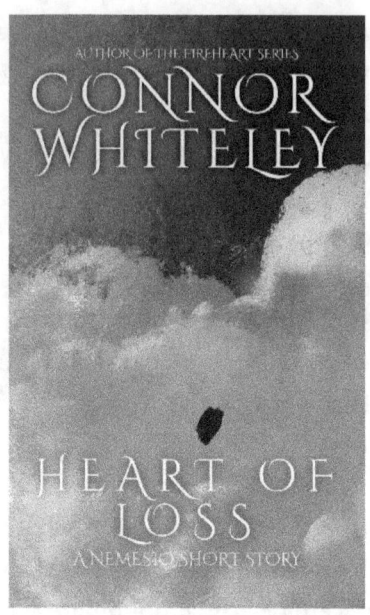

GET YOUR FREE AND EXCLUSIVE SHORT STORY NOW! LEARN ABOUT NEMESIO'S PAST!

https://www.subscribepage.com/fireheart

About the author:

Connor Whiteley is the author of over 60 books in the sci-fi fantasy, nonfiction psychology and books for writer's genre and he is a Human Branding Speaker and Consultant.

He is a passionate warhammer 40,000 reader, psychology student and author.

Who narrates his own audiobooks and he hosts The Psychology World Podcast.

All whilst studying Psychology at the University of Kent, England.

Also, he was a former Explorer Scout where he gave a speech to the Maltese President in August 2018 and he attended Prince Charles' 70th Birthday Party at Buckingham Palace in May 2018.

Plus, he is a self-confessed coffee lover!

OTHER SHORT STORIES BY CONNOR WHITELEY

Blade of The Emperor
Arbiter's Truth
The Bloodied Rose
Asmodia's Wrath
Heart of A Killer
Emissary of Blood
Computation of Battle
Old One's Wrath
Puppets and Masters
Ship of Plague
Interrogation
Edge of Failure
One Way Choice
Acceptable Losses
Balance of Power
Good Idea At The Time
Escape Plan
Escape In The Hesitation
Inspiration In Need
Singing Warriors
Dragon Coins
Dragon Tea
Dragon Rider
Knowledge is Power
Killer of Polluters

Climate of Death
Sacrifice of the Soul
Heart of The Flesheater
Heart of The Regent
Heart of The Standing
Feline of The Lost
Heart of The Story
The Family Mailing Affair
Defining Criminality
The Martian Affair
A Cheating Affair
The Little Café Affair
Mountain of Death
Prisoner's Fight
Claws of Death
Bitter Air
Honey Hunt
Blade On A Train
City of Fire
Awaiting Death
Poison In The Candy Cane
Christmas Innocence
You Better Watch Out
Christmas Theft
Trouble In Christmas
Smell of The Lake
Problem In A Car

Theft, Past and Team
Embezzler In The Room
A Strange Way To Go
A Horrible Way To Go
Ann Awful Way To Go
An Old Way To Go
A Fishy Way To Go
A Pointy Way To Go
A High Way To Go
A Fiery Way To Go
A Glassy Way To Go
A Chocolatey Way To Go
Kendra Detective Mystery Collection Volume 1
Kendra Detective Mystery Collection Volume 2
Stealing A Chance At Freedom
Glassblowing and Death
Theft of Independence
Cookie Thief
Marble Thief
Book Thief
Art Thief
Mated At The Morgue
The Big Five Whoopee Moments
Stealing An Election
Mystery Short Story Collection Volume 1

Mystery Short Story Collection Volume 2

Other books by Connor Whiteley:
Bettie English Private Eye Series
A Very Private Woman
The Russian Case
A Very Urgent Matter
A Case Most Personal
Trains, Scots and Private Eyes
The Federation Protects

The Fireheart Fantasy Series
Heart of Fire
Heart of Lies
Heart of Prophecy
Heart of Bones
Heart of Fate

City of Assassins (Urban Fantasy)
City of Death
City of Marytrs
City of Pleasure
City of Power

Agents of The Emperor
Return of The Ancient Ones
Vigilance

Angels of Fire
Kingmaker

The Garro Series- Fantasy/Sci-fi
GARRO: GALAXY'S END
GARRO: RISE OF THE ORDER
GARRO: END TIMES
GARRO: SHORT STORIES
GARRO: COLLECTION
GARRO: HERESY
GARRO: FAITHLESS
GARRO: DESTROYER OF WORLDS
GARRO: COLLECTIONS BOOK 4-6
GARRO: MISTRESS OF BLOOD
GARRO: BEACON OF HOPE
GARRO: END OF DAYS

Winter Series- Fantasy Trilogy Books
WINTER'S COMING
WINTER'S HUNT
WINTER'S REVENGE
WINTER'S DISSENSION

<u>Miscellaneous:</u>
RETURN
FREEDOM
SALVATION
Reflection of Mount Flame
The Masked One
The Great Deer

All books in 'An Introductory Series':
BIOLOGICAL PSYCHOLOGY 3RD EDITION
COGNITIVE PSYCHOLOGY THIRD EDITION
SOCIAL PSYCHOLOGY- 3RD EDITION
ABNORMAL PSYCHOLOGY 3RD EDITION
PSYCHOLOGY OF RELATIONSHIPS- 3RD EDITION
DEVELOPMENTAL PSYCHOLOGY 3RD EDITION
HEALTH PSYCHOLOGY
RESEARCH IN PSYCHOLOGY
A GUIDE TO MENTAL HEALTH AND TREATMENT AROUND THE WORLD- A GLOBAL LOOK AT DEPRESSION
FORENSIC PSYCHOLOGY
THE FORENSIC PSYCHOLOGY OF THEFT, BURGLARY AND OTHER CRIMES AGAINST PROPERTY
CRIMINAL PROFILING: A FORENSIC PSYCHOLOGY GUIDE TO FBI PROFILING AND GEOGRAPHICAL AND STATISTICAL PROFILING.
CLINICAL PSYCHOLOGY
FORMULATION IN PSYCHOTHERAPY

PERSONALITY PSYCHOLOGY AND INDIVIDUAL DIFFERENCES
CLINICAL PSYCHOLOGY REFLECTIONS VOLUME 1
CLINICAL PSYCHOLOGY REFLECTIONS VOLUME 2
CULT PSYCHOLOGY
Police Psychology

Companion guides:
BIOLOGICAL PSYCHOLOGY 2ND EDITION WORKBOOK
COGNITIVE PSYCHOLOGY 2ND EDITION WORKBOOK
SOCIOCULTURAL PSYCHOLOGY 2ND EDITION WORKBOOK
ABNORMAL PSYCHOLOGY 2ND EDITION WORKBOOK
PSYCHOLOGY OF HUMAN RELATIONSHIPS 2ND EDITION WORKBOOK
HEALTH PSYCHOLOGY WORKBOOK
FORENSIC PSYCHOLOGY WORKBOOK

www.ingramcontent.com/pod-product-compliance
Lightning Source LLC
LaVergne TN
LVHW011833060526
838200LV00053B/3995